Character and Situation

CHRISTOPHER SYKES

Character and Situation

SIX SHORT STORIES

INTRODUCTION BY EVELYN WAUGH

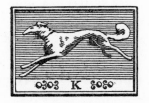

NEW YORK   ALFRED A. KNOPF   *1950*

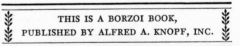

TO

Daphne

✳ *Introduction*

BY EVELYN WAUGH

THE ATLANTIC, across which politicians and commercial-travellers skim so swiftly, offers a stiffer obstacle to the artist. There is usually a lag of ten or twelve years before a European reputation reaches America. It would be superfluous and impertinent to attempt the introduction of Mr. Christopher Sykes to his own countrymen, who have long given him a warm corner in their esteem. But it appears that there are American readers who, in spite of the succes d'estime of "Four Studies in Loyalty," are still insufficiently informed about him.

Ladies and Gentlemen of the New World, let me present Mr. Sykes. You see before you a tall, rather carelessly dressed Englishman of early middle age. Twelve years ago you would have met someone young and bearded, but the war (in which Mr. Sykes served with distinction in a particularly daring parachute unit) has shorn his cheeks. He takes your hand with what may seem to be un-English effusiveness. He addresses you vivaciously, perhaps in theatrical tones, for it is one of his habits to assume a burlesque character at certain stages of his day. He will talk to you on whatever topic happens to be engaging him at the moment, probably one in which you have little interest — the character of some mid-Victorian prelate, or, maybe, a feature of Far-Eastern geography. He gives the impression of having ample leisure for this and other social activities, but he is a man of a double life, who contrives somehow, somewhere out of sight, to do a reasonable amount of conscientious research and literary composition.

Mr. Sykes was born in 1907, which is perhaps the last year in which a good Englishman could be born. In 1908 the Welfare State began under Asquith and Lloyd George, Post-Impressionism reared its frightful head, and a blight fell on the British Isles like phylloxera on the vineyards. The sturdier female stocks survived and you will find many excellent Englishwomen born after that date. But our manhood was struck hard and mysteriously. You will find many young men with virtues common to the other, lesser breeds, but you will not find genuine 100% Englishmen.

Mr. Sykes, as I say, was one of the last healthy batch. He comes of a line of sporting Yorkshire squires, who in the last generation became Catholic. That accounts for his untidy appearance which we have remarked above. It is not at all a symptom of Bohemian leanings: but of Benedictine education. Those holy, musical men in their shapeless habits, do not teach their little pupils how to dress. An English boy at a Protestant school starts — or perhaps I should say started — his day in early school under the liverish eye of his form master. (I daresay that nowadays he starts it on the psycho-analyst's couch.) At a Catholic school he starts it at Mass, in dim light, where he can tie his shoes and button his trousers and straighten his tie without detection. So Mr. Sykes, like all good Catholics, looks as though he had got up in a hurry.

From Downside he went to Oxford where the last of the healthy batch grew up in traditional ways. (After them came a rabble of politicians, and after them a herd of examinees.) From Oxford he passed into a world where it was still easy and agreeable to travel and he travelled widely. Englishmen were once the least insular of races. They went everywhere with a kindly curiosity and an instinctive, unquestioned conviction of total superiority. Thus, when the going was good, Mr. Sykes amassed the experiences that were to fit him to be a writer. He did not take a course in "Creative Writing": he lived; with the result that his first book of stories "Stranger Wonders" was written with great ease and maturity.

The stories presented here are typical of his talents. All have a foreign setting; all have great variety. If I had to name the particular qualities of his work I should put this, Variety, first. There are many writers who confine themselves to one narrow milieu and fret away, book after book, with its problems. Not so Mr. Sykes. Secondly, I should put Independence. He is obviously not writing for a particular market — the vice that has enervated so many modern writers. Thirdly, I should put something which it is not easy to define in a single word. It is almost the gift of seeing events "sub specie æternitatis." The tales are discursive and anecdotal but they each have a distinct, philosophic point; not exactly a moral, but a sense of human relations as existing on something higher than a social or sociological basis.

Introduction

Anyway, dear Ladies and Gentlemen of the New World, here he is for your enjoyment. Take him to your warm hearts. He is worthy of them.

EVELYN WAUGH

✻ *Foreword*

THE SIX COMIC STORIES which appear in this book contain no exact portraits from life among their characters.

As regards situations, these are fancied with the exception of that shown in the story called *The Sacred and the Profane*. I must say something about it.

Many soldiers who served in the Eighth Army during the advance from El Alamein, and some of the less noble fry who, like myself, were in the Cairo General Headquarters at that time, may remember an incident similar to what I describe here. I will not deny that that incident contains the origin of this story, but I will insist that the clash of personalities, on which the story turns, has been invented, and I have no evidence to make me suppose that I have guessed aright the course of events which led to that truly heroic episode. I stress this because when a shortened version of the story was broadcast, very ably, by Mr. Sebastian Shaw, several listeners, who had been with the Eighth Army aforetime, supposed that this entertainment was a detailed record of fact.

C. S.

Contents

Character and Situation

☆ *The Sacred and the Profane*

PATHOLOGICAL Chairmanship. This is my private term for a certain mental abnormality, and I call it by this name because I cannot discover the correct scientific description. I have often hunted for it in books of psychology, and it has sometimes seemed possible to me that the thing itself has been overlooked. If so, then I suggest that when they come to tackle it, as they must, psychologists use my term, for it is much better than the pedantic barbarisms which unfortunately are considered a necessary language in the science of the soul.

This pathological chairmanship is a phase of the mental temperament opposite to solitary contemplation; it describes the kind of mind which works best while presiding over a debate. It is rather the fashion nowadays to despise any sort of crowd-happy mind such as this, out of reverence, I suppose, for the sort which works best in lonely rapture, but, for all that, it is certain that these other gregarious people, of whom pathological chairmen form a large part, are in most cases people of powerful mental calibre. This was certainly true in the very extreme case of my friend Adrian Lally.

He was a fat and sensitive man, at once noble-minded

and worldly, a recent convert to Roman Catholicism who looked not unlike a portrait of Handel, unless you insisted on dowagers. He spoke with a slight lisp.

When I was sent to Egypt as a staff officer during the first part of the war, I was pleased to find that Adrian was one of my colleagues. I had grown attached to him in the course of ten years' acquaintance, and he seemed to like me very much in return. He occupied an office immediately below my own in that huge great horrible block of flats in Cairo, called "Grey Pillars," in which General Headquarters were housed from May 1940 onwards. It was here, sometime in 1942, that I finally discovered that Adrian was a pathological chairman.

I thought at first, with surprise, that he was a very lazy man, an incurable coffee-houser. Twice a week or more he would ask me to come down to his office (which was entirely separate from mine), where I would find a sort of committee assembled. I soon saw that this was a regular routine, and I also saw that he did not much mind who the members of his committee were; he simply wanted to collect people who were not too shy to express an opinion, and for this purpose almost any stray dog would do. This discovery decided me to give up attendance. If Adrian wanted to listen to nonsense to suggest the right idea to him, well, he could get it from someone else. I had not the time. But my friend was very angry with me when I no longer obeyed his summons and he fell into a thorough hobble-gobble temper when I told him why.

"You *are* a clever little delver into the mysteries of human nature, aren't you?" he said.

4

"Well, I've known you a long time."

He was much too good-natured to remain angry for more than a moment. He laughed at himself.

"All right, you can have that trick. But sometimes, you know, I really do need your advice, for its own sake, I mean, really, and on one subject above all."

"What subject is that?"

"The Church. . . . Oh, don't misunderstand me. I don't see a great spiritual force in you, my dear hog. Far from it. But you were born within the Church's bosom, whereas I was not. It excites me consciously, whereas to you it's familiar. To me it's my adorable new mother, to you it's your old aunt. I'm far more right than you about the important part, but you know the unimportant part better than I ever will. I hope you don't think I have spiritual pride."

"Spiritual pride is in the important part, so I wouldn't know. Do you really want my help?"

"I really do," he answered seriously. "Though it's nothing to do with me officially, the fact that I am well known as a Catholic gives me an enormous amount of additional, and sometimes painfully unpleasant extra work."

I understood what he was referring to. Very naturally the outbreak of war with Italy let loose some anti-Catholic feeling among the British. There was never a serious breach, nothing terrible happened, but there were many little irritating and threatening incidents, and these all found their way into Adrian's office.

"Tomorrow, for example," he said, "I have Father Macdonnel coming to see me. There's been some quite *appalling* ecclesiastical trouble in Mahammadieh. It's very shocking, so far as I can make out, so I don't want to ask anyone else, for fear of causing scandal. Can I rely on you for eleven o'clock?"

"I can't be with you before a quarter past. I'll come, though."

"You come."

I kept that appointment.

Father Macdonnel was seated on a chair opposite to Adrian. His eyes flashed fire, his lean neck was red with anger. He had apparently come to the end of a discourse.

"And I'm telling you, Colonel Lally," he was saying, "that it is a blasphemous and detestable occurrence to which I have been subjected, and I am demanding the strongest imaginable action by the Commander in Chief, both on behalf of myself, and of the chaplains under my command."

Adrian turned to me. "Here you are at last," he said. "Of course, you know Father Macdonnel."

I had met him several times before. He was the senior Roman Catholic chaplain in one of the corps of the Eighth Army, a position he disliked as it kept him at Headquarters, and he was a bold, adventurous man. When he first came to Egypt as a battalion chaplain he had the misfortune to become well known on account of certain acts of daring in the course of duty, and this caused the authorities to promote him to his present post for which he was not happily fitted. Office work, the dull duties of "welfare" organization, and so on, had a little soured his temper, and the outburst, of which I had

6

heard the concluding phrases, was characteristic of his changing nature. Irish bitterness was taking the place of Irish good-humour.

We shook hands for we had not met for some months, and I said I was very glad to see him again. Adrian pointed to a chair for me. He then opened the conference in a formal manner.

"Father Macdonnel has just come from Mahammadieh," he said, "which is Rear Headquarters of his corps for the time being. Things have been going badly, and the question is whether it would be a good thing to inform the Chief personally. Now, Father Macdonnel, if it is not too much trouble, would you repeat what you have just told me in the fullest possible detail for the benefit of our friend. I also would like to hear the facts again so as to get them straight."

As he pushed cigarettes in front of us Adrian caught my eye for a second, and I noted a look of fun. Father Macdonnel began his tale.

In time of war one gets so used to odd things that one's mind becomes like a bin; such quantities of queer trash are flung into it daily, to be emptied out later, that, in the way of bins, a beautiful jewel or other little masterpiece lies confused with the rubbish, and not noticed till later. It was not immediately that I recognized that Father Macdonnel's experiences at Mahammadieh were among very remarkable incidents of sacred history.

In those far-off days the name of Mahammadieh was heavily charged with emotion, it was the name of the second most important town in Italian North Africa. It had once been Italian Headquarters. The capture and loss of Mahammadieh under Sir Archibald Wavell, its recapture by Sir Claude Auchinleck, its loss again by us to Rommel in 1942, had all been occasions of extreme excitement, days bright with joy or black with bitterness. At the end of 1942 the place came into the news for the last time. General Montgomery, it will be remembered, attacked at Alamein, and on a great day less than a month later, poor Mahammadieh was liberated for good. There was no battle this time. The Germans and Italians retreated and we rushed in, and among the first on our side to head as fast as possible for this town was Father Macdonnel.

For him the place had special attractions. Among the monuments which the Italians had raised to their colonial rule was a Christian cathedral, a spacious handsome building, not very distinguished architecturally, but well proportioned, and supporting a large very well designed green dome. It was not a stupefaction of the world, as Italian propagandists used to say, but it was a civilized edifice. It conferred genuine dignity on Mahammadieh. To this church Father Macdonnel now sped in his fifteen hundredweight truck with holy zeal. He wanted to start religious services in it immediately, if possible so that not one day should elapse in which Mass had not been celebrated within its walls.

He arrived to find expected confusion. All the priesthood, except one, had left in panic. Between the retreat of the Axis army, and the arrival of our own, an interval of several hours had occurred during which there had been some abominable scenes of looting, nowhere worse than in this part of the town; indeed an effort had been made

8

to burn down the whole quarter. After looking round the littered streets Father Macdonnel went into the cathedral. He saw a hideous heap of smashed and upturned church furniture in the centre of the nave, and on this a group of about twenty British soldiers reclining in different attitudes of fatigue. Some of them were dozing. The wakeful ones were smoking. Military kit was strewn all over the floor and rifles piled against the high altar. In a dark corner, gibbering with fear, crouched the one remaining Italian priest, the aged sacristan, who had been left behind. He was simple, in the sense that his mental powers had degenerated into subnormality. Father Macdonnel watched him come out of his corner, and in pitiful fear, like that of an animal exploring some object of fascination and terror, hesitantly creep towards the soldiers, gaze at them with terror-wide eyes, and then appeal to them in broken accents and using pathetic gestures of beseeching. As the soldiers could not understand a word he said, they replied facetiously. "Keep yer 'air on, monkey fice," said one. "Give 'im a burst, Charlie," said another, and they used other less restrained expressions. The old man skipped back into his corner with a little squeal. The British Tommy's famous capacity to make friends with foreigners all the world over was momentarily suspended. It was a scene of loathsome sordidness.

Father Macdonnel swiftly corrected the situation. He started by ordering the men to remove their hats and put out their cigarettes, and after an hour or so he ended by rewarding them for their heavy labours by assigning them billets in two of the side chapels of the now thoroughly well-tidied fane. He gave them this shelter on condition that they behaved with scrupulous decency and left as soon as other accommodation was available. There was a look in his eye and something about his thin set mouth which made them obey him. Having settled the men, he began to inspect damage with the poor old bearded sacristan who was called Father Battino.

There was less than he had feared. True, a great many window panes were smashed; no lecterns remained; where, Father Battino assured him, there had been a silver offertory-stand by the high altar, there was now an ugly rent in the plaster; the golden door of the tabernacle, the rich sanctuary lamp, and the candlesticks, had been stolen; and in the sacristy many cupboards had been wrenched open and all the copes removed. The "treasure," the collection of monstrances and other sacred vessels presented by the King of Italy after the Lateran Treaty, and by other people on other occasions, had all gone too. The Germans had taken a good deal, but most of the looting had been done by the local people. At the end of their tour of inspection Father Battino sat down in the sacristy and wept bitterly; but Father Macdonnel stood fingering his chin and saying to himself: "Well now, it's not so bad as it might be. Not by any means."

The Sacrament had not been violated; it had not been removed by the runaways, but it had been well hidden away. The church linen, the chasubles, the stoles and maniples, had, rather inexplicably, escaped the notice of the looters, and, oddest thing of all, the altar wine was standing unhidden and unmolested in a corner. The looters were probably coming back for a final visit when the approaches to the cathedral from the poor quarters were blocked by the advancing army. A merciful chance. Father Macdonnel gave the sacristan a pull at his whisky flask and continued his inspection alone. Perhaps if he had not already found much to surprise him agreeably he would not have been so exasperated at the loss he now discovered. He returned to the sacristy after an intense search and addressed Father Battino. "Ubi Calix?" he asked in a rich brogue, "Where is the chalice?" for their conversation was conducted in the decadent Latin of the Roman Rite, in which language Father Macdonnel's Irish intonation was more noticeable than in English.

"Stolen! Stolen!" wailed the old man. "See, this is where the chalices were kept," and he tottered pointing to a splintered cabinet, "and there were other chalices here!" he whirled round and pointed to the battered treasure, "and they took the copes too, and the Holy Water stoup, and the Offertory-stand, and — "

"Yes yes, I know," said Father Macdonnel. "Repetare non est necessarium. *Who* took the chalices? That's the point."

"Tedeschi! Germani!" replied the sacristan.

"Oh." This was serious. "All of them?"

"All! All! Even the chalice which was used at Mass at the high altar yesterday morning. I myself saw an Arab running away with it." And with a fresh burst of tears he pointed to a small cupboard over one of the chests of drawers before which the priest is wont to vest himself for Mass.

"An Arab? Not a German?"

"No! No! An Arab!" cried the sacristan, wringing his hands, as though this made it a thousand times more frightful. "He came in all alone while the rest of his people were in the church, and he tore open the cupboard — like this — like a wild beast — and then he ran away with the chalice. I tell you I saw him! I saw him!"

Father Macdonnel sat down and went over this evidence carefully. He established that while all the other chalices had been taken by the Germans, this chalice, the one used at the high altar that day, had been stolen by a local man. He patted Father Battino on the shoulder and assured him that he would get the chalice back to the cathedral. He meant it, he believed it. Meanwhile, using his own battered mug-like field chalice, he said Mass in the cathedral next morning.

Father Macdonnel had an interpreter, a man called Attar, who accompanied him everywhere. I remembered Attar well, indeed his heavily charged breath, which contrasted so eerily with his name, was unforgettable, and it was through Attar that Adrian, for a little time, as though by a side door, made a minor but personal appearance in the story.

Why Father Macdonnel kept this man in his service was something of a mystery, unless you remembered the attraction that lost sheep have for holy people. He had been dismissed from a Greek cotton firm for peculation when he presented himself to Father Macdonnel as a persecuted Lebanese Christian thirsting to work for the glory of God. As with so many people of criminal character his cunning was inextricably mixed with stupidity, and on this occasion he had not troubled to find out whether Father Macdonnel knew Colonel Lally. He would have done well to investigate this matter as it contained seeds of disaster: a few months previously Attar had presented himself to Adrian as a Moslem grandee who knew every Muhammadan notable from King Ibn Sa'ud downwards. Adrian had dismissed him after a few weeks highly unsatisfactory service whence he had gone to the Alexandrian cotton business. Father Macdonnel was told all about this, but in vain. Because his nature was what it was, he conceived a sort of mad loyalty to this being. "I want an interpreter," he said, "not a virtuous man." Attar was without doubt a very gifted linguist. He could strip all beauty and poetry from at least five idioms. He could make French sound gross and Arabic insipid.

The day after their arrival in Mahammadieh, Father Macdonnel gave Attar his instructions. He was to lurk about the bazaars and find out what had become of the looted church property. He was to get the names of the looters and tell them to bring the stuff to the church. He could promise them rewards and no legal action against them.

"And how much dough am I empowered to promise these people, Sir?" asked Attar.

"You can tell them to come along at eleven on Sunday without fear," replied Father Macdonnel, "and I'll give them something out of the collection at Sung Mass."

"But these people will be at me for one Hell of a lot of cash, Sir."

"I dare say. I'm not here to subsidize sacrilege."

13

With a rather indefinite financial programme, there-fore, Attar sneaked off to the poorer quarters.

The bazaars, with their age-long romance of teeming swindle, were to Attar what hot-houses are to flowers of the equator. He did well there. Within three days he had obtained five candlesticks, the door of the tabernacle, a lamp which had been stolen from a private house (as was discovered much later) but which did good service in the sanctuary, and a number of other odds and ends from the great pillage. Attar, mingling promises with threats, got the looters to bring these things to the church. Then success, as usual, went to his feather-brained head, and before very long he was promising vast fortunes. The treasure began to flow back again, and several items had to be rejected by Father Macdon-nel as being by no conceivable probability part of the furnishings of a Christian place of worship. Father Mac-donnel calculated that within a week much more than half the looted property would once more be in the hands of the clergy. On Saturday the silver offertory-stand was returned.

Father Macdonnel was a straight and honourable man. In consequence he made a sorry mess of this business, because, once involved in a shady policy, he lost his way. He was short-sighted in crime. He made an idiotic error in promising this dividend on Sunday: a little thought should have made it clear to him that his interest lay in a firm refusal to pay anything until all the looted property was returned. But even in the performance of good works he was inclined to be impulsive and unreflective. He was lost here.

After Mass on Sunday he went to the sacristy door, as arranged. He found a vociferous and sweltering mob who had assembled on Attar's instructions. Attar himself stood in front of them with a hideous proprietary air, and he greeted the priest with a wave of his hand to this flock. "Here they are, Sir," he said.

Father Macdonnel surveyed them from the steps with a scowl.

"What do they want?" he asked.

"Why what the Hell d'ya think they want except to be paid up of course."

"These are the looters, are they?" the priest answered with affected surprise. "I see. Very well, give them twenty-five piastres apiece."

"Twenty-five piastres!" screamed Attar in horror, but before he could say more the priest, in order to forestall him, shouted in Arabic: "Twenty-five piastres!"

Immediately a suspicion of the ghastly truth as to how they had been tricked began to spread in the crowd. Many of them turned to Attar to demand what this meant, and Attar, after an unsuccessful attempt to parley with Father Macdonnel, who stood at the top of the sacristy steps looking on with icy contempt, repeated to them that their reward was to be twenty-five piastres each, which in those days was equivalent to five shillings.

"And hurry up and get on with it," added Father Macdonnel dramatically throwing a tied-up roll of notes to him.

There was something so awful in the priest's controlled anger that a hush came for a moment over the crowd.

Attar, with a worried expression, had actually begun to perform his task of distributing these paltry wages before he was brushed aside, while there arose a wild, loud, long wail, followed suddenly by another, deep, horrible, more savage noise — the voice of their loathing of the infidel Christian, the voice of Jahad or Holy War. One or two advanced to the priest with extended palms showing the little crumpled cheap bank notes which they had received in the place of expected millions. But Father Macdonnel raised his hand for silence, and through Attar spoke to them. They listened appalled at what he said.

If they thought they were merchants, he began, they were mistaken. They were looters. Their names had all been taken. It was not customary to reward looters but to punish them. Did they know what the punishment for looting was? It was — death. (He suspected, rightly, that Attar would not like to translate this, so he said it three times, and added some gestures.) Strictly, he went on, they were all under sentence. If there was one more word of complaint their names, all of them, would be given to the Military Police and there would be a mass execution. He had no more to say. The choice was theirs. He had spoken. A minute later dust rose high into the air. Without waiting for their money, with the rapid patter of the feet of fear, they rushed off to their houses and hid in them for the rest of that day and most of the next. Attar was worried.

"Why didn't ya let me speak to these damned natives, Sir?" he asked.

"Because I do it better," replied the priest angrily.

"You make one Hell of a mess of it, Sir. Who's going to sell me any church gadgets now, eh? You've killed the damned cow who lays the golden calf. You don't understand these bloody people, Sir."

"I'm not a Moslem if *that's* what you mean."

"No more am I a Moslem. Colonel Adrian Lally is one bloody big liar. He goes round Cairo crying out filthy things concerning me. Who the Hell says I am a Moslem?"

"You do when it suits you."

But Attar was quite right. Returns of church property dropped to nil immediately, the flow of sacred valuables had been turned off at the main, the spring had been parched by disappointment and fear, and the chalice, the chalice which without doubt was somewhere there in those filthy bazaars, had not been recovered. Father Macdonnel's irritation increased as he thought over this failure. His ultimate realization that, if he had followed Attar's advice, he would almost certainly have succeeded, was bitter in the extreme. Desperately he took to the bazaars himself. He strode about them with a black frown on his face; he glared and peered into every shop where a chalice might be hidden amid piles of junk; he yelled his sixteen words of Arabic into many a merchant's ear; he achieved nothing. At this point an important development began. Attar, once more took a hand in the search.

General Montgomery's advance was in full tide. Ten days after Father Macdonnel's arrival in Mahammadieh the rumble of the guns was no longer audible there, and from the poetry and squalor of the front line the town began to turn to the discomforts of restored life. It had been, comparatively speaking, mildly damaged in the campaign, and the army decided to use it as a convalescence and sick leave centre, of course on a modest scale. It had a good hospital, a few large hotels, and excellent sea bathing. It had once hoped to be a tourist-trap. As Mahammadieh remained the rear Headquarters of Father Macdonnel's corps, he was obliged to stay there until the next big leap forward in the advance, and so he was ordered to help his colleagues to found some sort of a troops' club. The chaplains had a great deal of work to do in devising from slender materials the means for men to enjoy themselves, nor were any of them particularly gifted in this task. Least of all Father Macdonnel. He was not interested in enjoyment. They were all much relieved when a regular "welfare" officer arrived from Cairo. For Father Macdonnel this meant, above all, that he could give more time to the restoration of the religious life of the cathedral, an undertaking where, in the midst of success, he was never for an instant unmindful of his one great failure: the absence of a certain chalice from the altar.

The welfare officer was an energetic and efficient man. He got a cinema going; he conjured up concerts and theatricals; he saw that the club was well stocked with newspapers, and tinned beer called Rheingold; and he organized a sports meeting. . . . At this sports meeting the main event was to be a horse race, and this horse race was to be run for a trophy, and the trophy was to be known as The Mahammadieh Cup. Father Macdonnel was invited to be a steward. The welfare officer was a very able officer indeed.

It was Attar who told Father Macdonnel that the chalice had been discovered. He told him that he had found the man who had bought it from the thief, and — here Attar looked suspiciously mournful — the man had unfortunately sold it to a British officer. Oh yes, he knew who the officer was, yes, he was in Mahammadieh. He was Major Swinstead. Swinstead was the name of the welfare officer. . . .

At the time when I heard this story from Father Macdonnel, I was puzzled by Adrian's signal to me with his eyes at the first mention of the horse race, and I would be happy indeed if I could convey to the reader the slow accumulation of enjoyment, the gradual and luxurious sinking into the pleasures of comedy which I experienced as the truth dawned on me. The Mahammadieh Cup and the chalice were one and the same.

"I took the sacristan round," said Father Macdonnel as he told the story, "I took him round and he identified it. Oh yes, he identified it. It was standing in Major Swinstead's office. There was no mistake in it. Attar had told me the truth. It was the cathedral chalice they were intending to run a horse race to win."

On the morning following this exposure Father Macdonnel sent round an early note to the welfare officer to say that he would call at ten-thirty on a most important matter. He would prefer to see him alone.

Had Attar remained away from the scene, there would have been a slender chance of the misunderstanding between the priest and Swinstead being arranged amicably, but unfortunately, at this moment, Attar, that cunning and foolish man, must needs try his hand at diplomacy.

Before that important ten-thirty he visited the welfare officer. He tried to frighten him. He told Major Swinstead how Father Macdonnel had summoned the people of the bazaars and threatened them with a massacre if all cathedral property was not returned immediately, and how he had personally ransacked several shops in search of the chalice, and how when he had heard that Major Swinstead had it in his possession he had broken into his office with the sacristan in order to make sure. "I tell you, Major Swinstead," he concluded, "that man is just raving crazy for his chalice. I warn you, Sir, not to make him more crazy. If you do I am damned well blowed if he will not seize the chalice by force and/or violence from you. I know bloody well indeed what I am speaking about."

Major Swinstead was one of those people who are easily liable to a sense of grievance. After Attar's visit he felt a very considerable sense of grievance. He was not a Catholic. In so far as he thought about religion he did so as a very pure Protestant. Though unacquainted with the term, he disliked ultramontanism, particularly since June 1940.

At half-past ten Father Macdonnel called on Major Swinstead. He was smiling and bent on good manners. He had forced himself to be optimistic about this matter. He was painfully aware of his faults of temper, and he was determined not to be unjust to Major Swinstead, who, after all, was entirely guiltless in what had happened.

"Good morning, Major," he said, "I hope I am not discommoding you, but you were good enough to ask me to be a steward at the races. . . . That is not a thing I believe I should do, strictly in accordance with Canon Law, but I think we may reasonably wave aside these objections in a place like Mahammadieh. Now, Major, I want to talk to you about this very horse race. It is about," and he shot a glance to the mantelpiece on which the chalice was standing, "the Cup."

Major Swinstead was a big fair man whose features in ill-humoured repose took on a look of obstinate surliness. On these occasions his voice sounded low and sullen, like the sound of a bell, the sort of bell, moreover, which might fittingly be hung in a large brick neo-Gothic clock tower in an English market square.

"What about the Cup?" he said.

Father Macdonnel caught the note of hostility.

"I should greatly like to know how you come to be in possession of that cup," he replied with a quick flash of anger in his eye.

"I bought it," said the Major, and gazed at him in the manner of some huge short-horn bull, as much as to say: "If you leave me alone you can quit the field without being gored."

Father Macdonnel started afresh. For the last time that morning he trod the path of appeasement.

"Well now, that's very understandable and I am sincerely sorry to have to cause you a great deal of disturbance and inconvenience. But the truth is, Major, that cup is church property. It is not a simple golden cup at all. It is a chalice. It is the cathedral chalice. It has been identified by Father Battino the sacristan — you know, the old man who remained behind — and strictly speaking it belongs to me, so long as I am here."

Major Swinstead's mouth became depressed as in an inverted smile; his face, including the lower of his two chins, became suffused with redness, in the midst of which his fair moustache seemed to sparkle like lightning flashes in sunset clouds. A wonderful sight.

"If you want," he said with slow and massive irony, "if you want to put in a claim that it's looted property, all right, well, and good. I'll forward it myself, and at the end of the war, or whenever Claims give you an authorization, the owner of the cup will give it back to you on receipt of compensation from the sub-department concerned. But my God," went on Major Swinstead, "coolly walking into my office and just bloody well ordering me to hand over the cup . . . And not only that. Coming along with this bloody Battino or whatever he's called and breaking into my office when I'm not there. Turning my whole office upside down. Bursting into my office as if it was a bloody thieves' kitchen. And then coolly walking into my office and demanding my property. Honestly, padre, I think that's the bloody limit." Major Swinstead had those extraordinarily morbid feelings of affection and loyalty towards the room where he conducted business which are so common in any form of official life, and particularly in the army.

Father Macdonnel turned on Swinstead in a passion of vehemence.

"You are talking like an uneducated child. Breaking into your office, my goodness! As a steward I have a right to see the cup, and I saw it. The door was open. As a priest I have a duty to identify sacred property and Father Battino has enabled me to identify it. You ought to be ashamed of yourself, Major Swinstead, talking so to me. You say I walk in and demand your property. I have not done so but I will do so now. I tell you that that cup is my chalice and I have a right to demand my chalice. And I do demand it. I demand that you hand over that cup, Major Swinstead. Do you understand that!"

"I bought that cup," said Major Swinstead, "and I won't hand it over unless I'm ordered to. That cup," he went on, "cost me a bloody lot of money. I can get some of it back, I dare say, but it was a bloody expensive cup. It isn't a lot of fellows who'd pay up more than they can afford with only an outside chance of a rebate, so's the chaps'll have a decent cup to race for. I'm not complaining. I'm simply trying to tell you that I'm not going to give up that cup, church property or no church property, no matter what you, and no matter what Father Bloody Battino, or anybody bloody else says, unless I'm ordered to by the Corps Commander or my senior officer in Cairo."

Father Macdonnel then posed him a serious question.

"Do you realize, Major Swinstead, that to Roman Catholics that cup is as sacred as any material object can be?"

Major Swinstead replied simply: "I'm not a Roman Catholic."

A gulf yawned. Two mighty antagonists faced one another. Major Swinstead was lost in the immense and ghostly company which drew up by his side; the fires of Smithfield roared round him. From him at that moment came the cry of freedom against priestly tyranny, against profitable superstitions, against worldly trafficking in holy things. His voice was the sublime utterance of the English Bible. His strength was the strength which had cast forth the ghost of the Roman Empire sitting crowned on the ruins thereof. And on the other side was unforsaken faith great in rule, and in constancy amid the grief of misfortune as the things of this world are reckoned. The ghosts of More and Campion stood there, and of another company, who had scorned peace and wealth at the price of Irish apostasy. The most superb of all claims fortified Father Macdonnel. "Upon this rock I will build My Church."

There was no more to be said. Father Macdonnel rose to his feet.

"I will refer this matter elsewhere," he said, and stalked in white fury out of the Welfare Office.

Heroic moments beget their contraries: moods of high passion often give way to moods of inventive common sense. As he walked out of Major Swinstead's office Father Macdonnel was in a state of exalted anger in which he felt he could have passed through the torture of martyrdom with defiant joy, in which the blows of chains would have felt like the blows of feathers. But when he arrived at the cathedral he was in a perfectly calm and practically inclined state of mind. He had said he would refer this matter elsewhere. He would indeed, and not first to the Corps Commander. A terrible smile crept over his thin mouth. He summoned Attar to his little office by the sacristy, and together they were long in conference. When Attar left, Father Macdonnel sent a curt note to Major Swinstead saying that he was not able to act as a steward for the forthcoming races.

"Bloody difficult chap, this R.C. padre," said Major Swinstead in the mess. "First he wants to pinch our cup and now he won't act as a steward."

"Funny," said his friend, "I'd have thought he was a sportsman."

The great day came, and every one, by which I mean more than half of the local people, the entire staffs of the various Headquarters, the wounded who could move, and the convalescents, two battalions who were in transit to the front line, and a hundred or so on sick leave, went to the racecourse. There was a greater crowd than had been seen there before in its short history. The sports began at three. The egg and spoon races, the three-legged races, the race for men dressed as women, the hurdles, the camel race, the donkey race, and the auction for a military charity of a case of Chianti wine, went well enough, went, all of them, as the frivolous overture before the performance of the great piece: the Mahammadieh Cup. A cab race had been suggested but it was pointed out that all but a few of the cab horses of the town had been entered for the main event.

The racecourse at Mahammadieh where this sporting festival took place is well designed. It was once madly hoped that horse racing would be one of the main attractions beckoning to tourists across the world, as is the case in Cairo. There is a paddock, an enclosure, a grandstand, and even a totalizator, though unfortunately the latter had recently received a direct hit, having been taken from the clouds for an important military installation, which, for all one knows, it might have been in the insanely practical way of warfare. This mattered little, however. There were bookmakers in the army, and they proclaimed themselves in many parts of the course. Newmarket sprung up like a mushroom in this oasis of Libya. Somebody rang a bell for saddling. When he rang it again five minutes later, a string of horses processed from the stables behind the paddock, each one saddled, and led by a native of the town, except one. This was a nicelooking half-Arab, very much the superior of the others. Arab is a loose term which covers many obscure breeds outside Arabia, but what was noticeably non-Arabian about this particular horse was its size, and a certain easy swing in its gait. It was led by Attar.

Before the bell rang again there was much cheering and jeering as the jockeys entered the sacred ring. Their caps and jackets were surprisingly professional in appearance and cut, but white breeches and mahogany-topped boots were in all cases substituted by khaki trousers fastened at the knee. It was amazing, so I was told by a man who was present, to see how exactly like an English race meeting this farcical competition became. The local people represented the dense noisy crowd, the densest and noisiest of all English crowds, the officers and men on leave became the counterparts of the privileged of the enclosures, and one could see instinctively how this man wore his white top hat at Ascot, or how that one with a bowler tilted forward over his brow, stood in impressive and secret preoccupation on the racecourse at York, which is pleasantly called the Knavesmire. The Corps Commander, who had flown over from forward Headquarters, for there was a lull in the advance, made a fitting Lord Lonsdale. Major Swinstead deputized for the clerk of the course.

The riders stood in the ring discussing last minute instructions with their patrons, as is the custom. Only one stood apart. He appeared on the card as E. Macdonnel. He ground his teeth. He was reflecting that for a priest to dress up in this clownish costume was very nearly sacrilegious in itself. Supposing . . . no, he would not toy with that appalling possibility. He had some faith in Attar's researches into the past racing history of Mahammadieh. He had yet more faith in his own eye for a horse. He had another faith too which exalted him. He wished the "jockeys up" bell would ring and hasten the end of this blasphemous farce.

The Corps Commander came up to him.

"Well, padre, this is a surprise seeing you here. Very sporting of you. Jolly good." He laughed.

"Thank you, Sir." He was tempted to tell him precisely why he *was* there. With blazing eyes he looked at the general, but controlled his feelings.

"Nice horse you've got too. Looks as if he's got some breeding."

"I selected him with care, Sir. I believe him to be a quarter bred, and if that is true it will be by Gay Crusader by the ugly look of him." As Father Macdonnel said this he looked at the horse again. There is a kind of equine ugliness which is enjoyable because, as they say in horsy language, it "fills the eye."

"I'll back you, padre." The general chortled with delight.

"You might do worse, though the horse is not young," replied Father Macdonnel who was not joining in the general's amusement.

"By Jove, he stands out, doesn't he? How did you find him?"

"My interpreter assisted me. We borrowed him from one of the shaykhs who used to race here. The man has removed what he could from the town as he knew the Germans were leaving. They told him. What other race-horses were here are either killed or as yet untraced, as the thieves are still hiding the live ones. There was much looting and disorder, you may recall, Sir." The Corps Commander discerned a note of sudden irritation in Father Macdonnel's last words. This puzzled him. Perhaps he imagined it.

"How d'you know the horse's breeding?"

"He was bought by Marshal Balbo from an Egyptian, who specializes in cross-breeding with Arab mares, for what they call country-bred racing."

The bell rang.

"Ah, you Irish! You can't keep away from a horse, can you?" He held up a finger waggishly. The priest did not smile.

"I have ridden very little since I took orders. . . . If you'll excuse me, Sir, I must mount."

"Good luck, padre."

28

There was a parade of horses on the course before the start. One of the first things to be noticed was how one or two horsemen stood out by reason of their professional style, and on the strength of it, number eighteen, E. Macdonnel up, became the favourite. When the beast cantered by the enclosure, wagging his head and lashing with his tongue, the odds on him shortened by yet another point. There were thirty-four in the field.

Starting was difficult because professional starters are rarer than other officials of the turf and there had been no time for experiments or rehearsals on an adequate scale. The starting gate, therefore, was handled in a clumsy manner. The proverb about too many cooks and broth applied well here: the gate was for ever going up and down, and there was a moment when a horse was swept off its hooves which were entangled in the strings. After this the gate was abandoned for the old-fashioned flag. There were six false starts from which several horses never returned. When they did get away number eighteen was last.

With few exceptions the riders flogged their horses into maximum speed from the beginning. Not so E. Macdonnel. It would be inaccurate to say that he rode a waiting race; he rode a professional race. His first object was to keep in the running, holding his horse for a final turn of speed, though beyond a general belief in the power of heredity, he had no means of knowing whether this turn was to be found in the descendant of Gay Crusader. He hoped so and guessed so. The race was ambitious: two miles and a half long. There were many distractions. At the seventh furlong one horse fell down dead. Half a furlong on another crashed into the rails at the bend. E. Macdonnel did not so much fear being shut in as being confused by dizziness from the zigzag path of the horses before him. His chance came at the last corner, a little under a mile from home. Here, while he hugged the rails, the whole field lurched over in a body to the far side, and another sickening splintering crash made him suppose, rightly as it happened, that yet another horse had been thrown off the course through the rails. A sharp competitor, ridden by a steeplechase jockey of former days, was coming up on his right. When he heard that approaching noise he at last liberated the all-necessary turn of speed, on which everything depended. It was there. It was not a great turn of speed, but it was there. He heard the horse on his right blow up with a very audible explosion, while his own horse settled into a heavy slogging gallop. It was not a fast horse. It was not a born winner. He heard another coming up behind him. He applied the whip. He spurred with his heels. But no tortures on this earth could accelerate the speed. The other horse drew near him, on his right again, but before it was abreast it also exploded. The descendant of Gay Crusader was a stayer, that was wonderfully clear. E. Macdonnel continued to apply the whip but without avail, only the heavy slogging gallop went on, at a regular speed. But it did go on. It went on and on and on. He was aware of a noise of cheering all about him. He saw the post ahead, and riding as though he was trying to strike out of a dead heat, Father Macdonnel won the Mahammadieh Cup by fourteen lengths. Ad Majorem Dei Gloriam.

When the cup was presented to Father Macdonnel by the Corps Commander, Major Swinstead came forward, beaming with admiration. Though he looked rather like a clock tower he was a warm-hearted man. But something in Father Macdonnel's expression warned him not to chaff or joke about this matter. The major held out his hand. Father Macdonnel took it in his own. This was not a reconciliation, it was a temporary act of fellowship in honour of the human virtues which show in sportsmanship. The gulf yawned as wide as ever, a bridge had been built sufficient for one passage only. And so the two men shook hands.

"And there," concluded Father Macdonnel, "you have the whole story before you. That is the naked fact, told without prejudice, and that is the case I wish your assistance in to lay personally before the Commander-in-Chief, so as to avoid the scandal of a whole lot of people hearing it in the usual channels."

The solution was perfectly simple to us, and we exchanged a look.

"Well," said Adrian to me, "and what do you suggest?"

I said the obvious thing which I believed to be the right thing: "I should leave it where it is, because to guard against the future seems to me such a waste of time here. I cannot believe that this sort of thing happens very often, and Father Macdonnel has got the chalice."

There was a short pause. Adrian slowly nodded his head to show he approved of what I had said.

"I should like to agree with you," answered the priest, "but this is a matter of principle."

Adrian signalled me again by his flirtatious dowager's eye. "Go on. Keep it up."

"Father Macdonnel," I said, "surely it is true that the principle has been vindicated in the most remarkable way possible."

As Father Macdonnel thought over my last words his mouth formed into a hard downward-pointing smile. "No," he said, "I cannot accept that explanation, much as I would like to. You are suggesting miracles, are you not? There was nothing miraculous about this horse race. Indeed this race was the very opposite of an occasion of grace — can you think of anything less edifying than that the clergy should compete like jockeys for sacred vessels? I think any right-minded spectator will have been utterly disgusted by this exhibition if he knew what was really taking place."

Though I knew that I was arguing against a wall, I went on: "No one does know what was really taking place. No one except Major Swinstead and Father Battino."

"And Attar," said Father Macdonnel.

At this moment, which I thought signalized the end of the contest, Adrian broke in at last. The chairman had woken up from his trance, and he brought his hand down on the table with a slam. "Attar," he said.

We both turned towards him.

"Attar," he said again, "he's the man. He's the solution. This is really much simpler than I thought. Attar has an abandoned Moslem wife who came to me for help a little time ago, and she told me a great deal about his spiritual experiences. Attar was born a Maronite Christian in the Lebanon and apostatized to Islam, when he went into the service of one of the Egyptian princes here, when he was a young man. He was back in Syria, about ten years ago, and then, until he was sacked for the usual peculations, he became secretary-general to the Atheist Youth Society of Syria and the Lebanon, in Beirut. That was his last change of faith which had any element of permanence about it. Since then, as you know, he dodges between the Cross and the Crescent in accordance with the fluctuations of the market. You may wonder what is the significance of this to your case. Believe me, it is immense. Tell me, Father, does Attar attend Mass when he goes round with you?"

"Yes."

"To impress *you*, I suppose."

"I am afraid that is his chief aim."

"I went to High Mass in St. Joseph's yesterday morning. After Mass, as the congregation was going out, I noticed something familiar by the main door. Attar had attended Mass, and not just to impress *you*, for once. And Attar paused at the box for the upkeep of the services, and he put in what looked to me like a hundred piastre note. Not a large part, I dare say, of what he made out of the chalice, but generous by his standards. Father Macdonnel, I would not dismiss the earlier suggestion of miracles. You may win a race by your own exertions, but you don't reclaim Attar that way."

There was a long silence. Father Macdonnel, I could see, was moved.

He got up to his feet. "Well, Colonel Lally," he said. "You know GHQ better than I do, so I will take your advice and not approach the Commander-in-Chief. Thank you for your trouble, both of you. Good morning." He marched out of the office.

Adrian and I often used to discuss that conference afterwards, and we used to invent such elaborations on Father Macdonnel's story that I find it difficult, at this distance of time, to set them aside from the precise truth. I believe I have succeeded nevertheless. I do not know what epilogue there was with Attar's wife as heroine, but the fact that there was neither a scandal nor any reappearance among us of Madame Attar suggests happy endings. Any happy ending to a story with which Attar was even distantly connected, must have been directly fashioned by powers greater than man.

✤ Saint George

I WISH I could play the piano. I ask for very little. I do not ask for extraordinary talent — far from it; I only want to be able to play a great many pieces from beginning to end. I once read in a novel of a man, an efficient piano-player, who had a feeling for music which was so exquisite that he would never play himself. His own performance fell too far beneath his standard, and gave him too much pain. I think that in his treatment of this subject the author showed very inaccurate observation: I am sure that my own case is far more classic: I am very easily put out by bad playing, and yet I find pleasure in playing very badly, myself to myself, and I am only sorry that I can play so little.

Since my undergraduate days I had wished to visit the little known Indian sub-province of Siwandistan, which neighbours the Afghan frontier; and at length, fifteen years ago, after much intrigue and importunity, I got a visa. In those days such visas had to be obtained at one or other of the few Consulates attached to British Legations in the East which were empowered to handle the interests of this little semi-independent principality. I speak of a now vanished age.

35

Within Siwandistan travel was most easily done on horseback, for the roads were neither straight nor smooth; indeed the first car which I saw after I had entered was after a ride of nearly two hundred miles, at Mashad Islam, a town about eighty miles from the borders of the North West Frontier Province. I was tired of the romance of out-door life by the time I reached this place, and so I made directly for a little caravanserai which had been partly converted into a garage. It was a picturesque building with thick mud walls and turrets mouldering and cracked by heat, and the stench of horse-dung and petrol all about it, like a hundred thousand such beggarly places; but to me, in my then state, the sight of a broad metalled road coming up to it, a great pile of empty petrol tins, and petrol advertisements, and a large lorry standing by the main gate; the sight of these things I welcomed, even with emotion, as the outstretched hand of my own bad world. I walked up to the building and saw a man sitting in front of the door on the remains of a European chair, and as I made my way across the large hot square which separated the town from the caravanserai I had time to notice his appearance. His face was red and though none of his hair was showing I saw that he was fair. I wondered whether he was of that race of fair pagans, the Kafirs, who live near here, and who are supposed to be descended from the Macedonians. His dress suggested a semi-Europeanized Pathan. He wore a waistcoat and shirt but no collar and tie, and the tails of his shirt, which was a European one, hung outside his trousers. The latter were white ducks with a blue stripe, greasy and very dirty, and I imagined that the ends of them were much frayed for he wore them inside his socks. He wore sock suspenders also and cracked brown shoes and on his head a turban, in the Pathan style, cocked forward towards one eye. I hoped he could tell me something about cars, and as he had about him the air of having come up the road from India proper (he was smoking a cigarette in a Western way), I said to him in English:

"Can you tell me how I can arrange for a lift in a lorry down to Jaideri?"

As he looked up at me I saw that his eyes were blue. He answered in perfect English:

"How much luggage have you got?"

"Three kitbags."

"Well, I'm going this afternoon."

"What'll you take me for?"

"It's a hundred and ten miles. I'll do it for sixty rupees."

"Sixty rupees! That's a lot."

He looked up at me smiling and blew out a cloud of cigarette smoke. There was a roguish good humour in his face which took any offence out of what he next said:

"And there're a hell of a lot of cars going from here to Jai' aren't there?"

I laughed: "Don't you ever bargain?"

"Pretty well all day long. Well, I'll throw in your baggage free."

I had never supposed that he intended to charge me for this. He went on: "Then we'll both be pleased. Do you agree?"

37

"Oh yes, I agree." I sighed. "I'll have the baggage here in half an hour. Will that do?"

I was bitten by fleas, I was debauched with adventure, and I longed for baths and beds and chairs. I was so tired that my brain was working more slowly than usual. I still presumed, from the evidence of his dress, that this lorry driver was some sort of Pathan. He answered:

"That'll do fine. You can sit in front with me. I'll make you comfortable."

"So you ought at the price I'm paying."

"Oh, that's all right. We'll stuff the wogs behind with the baggage, but we may have to squeeze a Pathan in front from time to time, if they grumble. They're not so easily put down as Indians."

It was only now that I realized that he was an Englishman. As he gave me a cigarette and I lit it I told him my name and asked him his:

"My name's Bishop," he said.

I brought my baggage round after half an hour or so, and at about two o'clock in the afternoon, we were ready to start. The lorry was crammed with baggage, and Indians, and Pathans, the largest and most heavily armed of whom sat in front with Bishop and myself. We were jammed together in a tight heap. Then we started on our bumpy dusty and slow journey. The noise of the engine overcame the din of the chattering passengers behind us, and so the Pathan and Bishop and I, thus separated from them, were left to our mutual studies. The noise of the engine was terrific and to make ourselves heard we had to shout. The Pathan addressed himself to me, offering me a cigarette, and smiling like a child behind his Hindenburg moustache. I roared to him, in Persian, that I did not speak the Pathan language, which is called Pushtu, and he answered me in a few broken words, but with the same childlike smile and hanging his head on one side, giving me to understand that he did not know Persian. Thereafter our intercourse was confined to huge smiles expressive of our immense esteem of each other, and after a little while the Pathan began to converse with Bishop. Although for some reason the English in England are not encouraged to learn foreign languages, they are, as anyone who went to India soon discovered, among the best linguists of Europe. But they nearly always speak foreign languages as though fully conscious that they are outlandish modes of expression. Bishop, on the other hand, spoke Pushtu in a manner quite indistinguishable from that of a Pathan. He spoke as fast if not faster than our companions; only his laugh was English, and my two companions laughed a great deal together; but the gestures of his hand, the way he laid his fingers on his breast and turned up his eyes at a compliment, the way he lolled back his head in the negative gesture, and the way in which, when there was a long silence between them, he sang in a high soft voice — the most polished actor could never have so exactly reproduced the original.

As might be imagined I was somewhat left out of the conversation, and I did not establish myself in it until about half-past four when we stopped at a little place called Shabbareg in order to take in some more petrol. There was a coffee-house by the garage and I sat on the end of the low bench with Bishop and the Pathan, and when the latter had drunk a cup of tea he walked off. Bishop turned to me and winked: "This is where he leaves his gun."

"You mean he'd get into trouble if he was found with it over the frontier?"

"That's right. And he's not the kind of chap who gets a licence."

"Shady character is he?"

"Siwandi Pathan. Same thing." He laughed to himself, enjoying the joke greatly. About twenty men and small children were standing in front of me, gazing at my European clothes. Bishop, suddenly noticing them, uttered a curse, and they walked away rapidly. My slow tired brain understood why he wore Pathan dress. He turned to me: "Are you an archaeologist?" he said.

"No. Why do you ask?"

"I wondered what you were doing here."

"I've been in Afghanistan with a friend of mine getting photographs of buildings for a survey. I had a visa for Siwandistan so I came down this way from Turkestan instead of by Kabul and the Khyber Pass."

"Have any trouble?"

"What sort?"

"Usual sort." He answered with a kind of conspiratorial smile. I did not quite understand what he meant.

"Brigands? As every one looks like a brigand in a pantomime I got used to them."

"And they don't only look like brigands; they are brigands." And he gave me the same deep smile.

During the rest of the journey the Pathan sat smoking and singing to himself while I talked to Bishop. He told me the story of his life. In 1914 he had joined up. He knew everything about cars and was a good mechanic and engineer. He was sent out to Egypt and then to Basrah and took part in General Maude's advance up the Tigris, and later served under Allenby in Palestine. He was in hand-to-hand fighting. He was given a commission and very nearly rose to the rank of Captain, so he gave me to understand, and was awarded the M.C. When the war was over he knocked about Egypt looking for work, and from the way he spoke of those days, with a melancholy laugh and the smallest touch of bitterness, I found it easy to picture a life of nerves not easily adjusted to relaxed tension, and rowdy parties in hotels, and desperate efforts to keep up the epic companionship of war now that its dangers had gone, and a gradual dissolution of these pleasures. He had at last got a job in some trading firm in Cairo and they sent him out to their branch in India. I cannot remember whether he told me, or whether I received the impression from hints in his narrative, that this firm eventually decided that he was too wild and odd a fellow to be advantageously employed by them. But they did not behave ungenerously, as the managing director of their Peshawar branch himself helped him with funds to start his own enterprise. The enterprise was one of transport: he bought four lorries which carried down charcoal from Siwandistan to Jaideri and Peshawar. I gathered that his partner in this concern, an Anglo-Indian, had "let him down." He had sold the business to a larger company, of whose Siwandistan branch he was now the managing transport director. He spoke with bitterness, and self pity. I was able to share the pity spontaneously. He seemed to be a very talented man, who, with few advantages, had worked his way up in the world, only to find himself too exhausted by the climb, and the world too unfriendly, to allow him to stay on the heights. The war had destroyed him. Quite obviously it remained in the centre of his thoughts and had conditioned him. As he drove he pushed his turban back from his forehead and I could see his face, clearly and in full. He had, as I had suspected, fair hair, and his eyes were of a quite theatrical blue, and they blazed out of his red complexion. He was thin, hard, and evidently very "fit." As a boy he must have been remarkably good looking, but his face had not matured; it had an appearance of raddled shattered youthfulness, and his protruding "cheeky" underlip, his strong jaw, and his long nose had all become too prominent. The sadness which seemed to haunt him had not quite hidden the fact that once he had been a rattling good fellow. I liked him, but I could see too that he was rather an irritating man.

When we reached Jaideri late that evening we said good-bye and promised to meet again soon.

It is now that I come to the piano, for it was owing to the piano that I came to be on terms of some intimacy with Vereker, and Vereker is the next personage of this story. I must explain first how I came to meet the piano. I knew one person in Jaideri and this was Mrs. Homer, the wife of an archaeologist. I had known her five years before in London, before she married. I was looking forward to seeing her once more but as I did not know her address in Jaideri, I had not warned her of my arrival.

Not vainly, I hoped, I enjoyed the thought of her coming surprise. As soon as I arrived I found a room in a hotel, and in the morning I went to the chief bank in order to find out the address of my friend. I arrived at the counter, I leaned across it, I asked if the clerk could tell me where Mrs. Homer lived, when a woman standing next to me said:

"Excuse me, did you say you are a friend of Mrs. Homer?"

"Yes, that's right," I told her my name. "I heard that she lived here and I thought I would stop and see her on the way to Bombay."

"That's too bad. You see she and her husband are away in the North somewhere digging," she flapped a gloved hand at the clerk. "That's all right," she said, and then to me: "My name is Mrs. Featherstone. Where have you come from?"

I outlined to her my immediate past, in which I mentioned the name of the friend whom I had left in Afghanistan. She seemed interested. "My husband is C.O. here," she said. "He knows Afghanistan very well. He reads your friend's books and likes them just immensely. I wonder if you would come and dine with us tonight? You see, we don't have many visitors," she added with a delightful chuckle at her naïve truthfulness. And then she added, "It's too bad your missing Mrs. Homer."

"I'm disappointed not to see her. But it's kind of you to ask me to dinner. I'd love to come. I'm afraid I can't dress."

"Why, don't let that worry you," she said with a smile. "I'll send round one of my husband's suits to your

43

hotel." And while I was still gasping at the formalism of English life in India, she produced a few more samples. "And we'll send round the automobile, and here's my card. And now I must rush. You are staying at the Jubilee Hotel, you said?"

"Yes, I am."

"Well, we'll just love seeing you at eight-thirty." And she bustled off. She was a woman of about fifty, very well dressed (which was a rarity in India), and she had about her a great air of fussy benevolence. The word "automobile" alone made me realize that she was an American, for her speech had little trace of American intonation, and that her magnificence might not be a native product of our Empire after all. The evening suit, with starched accompaniments, came round, and at eight o'clock a large car driven by two men in turbans. I was taken to the Commanding Officer's large hideous comfortable bungalow. A bearded retainer told me that the mem-sahib was not yet down but would I wait, and he ushered me into the drawing-room. I noticed that it contained a piano.

When I was alone, I tiptoed to the piano, and very softly I played something which bore a ludicrous resemblance to the Overture to Act III of the *Meistersinger*. I stopped and looked round. I was still alone. My enjoyment made me bold. I played a tune based on an aria in the St. Matthew Passion and when that became a little elaborate for me I fell to rumbling out the chords of an easy continuo and from this worked down to the key of G in which I played a nightmare version of the slow movement of the Seventh Symphony which I worked into the second movement of Beethoven's last Sonata. When I found myself in a suitable key I dashed off a passage of Bach's Toccata in D Minor and ended with the final chords of the *Rheingold*. I stopped, happy. At that moment Mrs. Featherstone came in. But she looked past me and said: "Oh, Tom, I hope you haven't been waiting a terribly long time." Then a voice behind me answered: "Rather not, I was listening to the piano."

I rose to my feet and turned round. I said, "Good evening" to Mrs. Featherstone. "It's terribly nice of you," she said, "to play my piano. I never knew — and so you two men have met."

"Well, no. I — "

"Oh, then I must present you to Major Vereker," and she introduced us. I held out my hand to the man who had overheard my shocking self-revelation, but he took it with a show of friendliness.

"I didn't want to disturb you playing," he said with no hint of sarcasm.

At that moment General Featherstone came in and when I had been introduced to him his wife told him that I played the piano quite beautifully. "Good Lord! Can you play the piano?" he said. "Do sit down and play some more."

"Well, really, you know, I hardly play at all."

"He plays *beautifully*, George!"

"Well after dinner, then. That's a bargain," said the General. Another bearded man wearing a spectacular turban came in with cocktails and I was safe for a little while.

Vereker looked about forty-five years old; lean, clean

45

shaven, and with thin well-brushed greying hair. His appearance was like that of a barrister, particularly when he wore his horn-rimmed glasses. The character of his face was very much that of the ascetic, the man capable of sustained mental work, the "sound" judge of numerous high specialties. In contradiction to his hard style, his lips were full and his mouth wide and going well into his flesh at the corners. It suggested that he had a great sense of humour, though when I came to know him, I found that he had little. He talked in a dry way but with such exactness that you were not bored, and he rarely went outside his own considered subjects. He was a political officer in the district. His triumph, so I was told later by Mrs. Featherstone, was the suppression of illicit trade, particularly of the illegal selling of guns to brigands and rebellious tribes in the Afghan frontier region and Siwandistan. I was naturally afraid that, only knowing me in my character of pianist, he would look upon me as a fool. But he was very friendly.

We dined, a party of five, for an aide-de-camp joined us, and while Vereker and the General tried but failed in the attempt not to talk shop, I talked to Mrs. Featherstone. Her attitude towards India was more like that of a tourist than of an official's wife forced into the scene of her husband's labours, and so she did not "go on" about India in the plaintive manner of many of her kind. She enjoyed the place. I liked her for that, I liked her in any case. We talked about Mrs. Homer, and I asked about Homer whom I had only met once.

When dinner was over we all went into the drawing-room. The General said: "Well, what about bridge!" to which his wife exclaimed: "But poor Tom doesn't play bridge." And the General replied: "Tom tells me he would like to read a file." Mrs. Featherstone then said: "Does the poor man really want to do anything so gloomy!" At this moment I was aware that Vereker was looking at me very hard. I met his eyes for a moment, and then he said to Mrs. Featherstone: "Yes, that's what I want to do." The file was got for him, and he sat down in an arm-chair to read. The Featherstones and the aide-de-camp (who looked like a greyhound) and myself sat down to bridge. I was saved. They had forgotten about the piano. And so the evening passed pleasantly enough. Vereker sat in an arm-chair smoking a pipe and reading a file, and after we had played three rubbers and rose up to drink whisky and soda he continued sitting there deeply absorbed. He was evidently not a sociable man.

He did not get up until it was time to say good-bye. Mrs. Featherstone asked me whether I would not like to be taken back to my hotel in her car, but Vereker offered to drop me. Then he told the General he would return the file in the morning, shot out his hand to Mrs. Featherstone saying, "Good night," and left, followed by me. As we drove in his open car through the wide balmy streets he said to me: "I wish I could play the piano."

"So do I."

"You can. You're lucky. You were taught as a boy, I suppose."

"Yes."

He was smoking a cigarette and he looked up reflectively, half-closing his eyes to the smoke. "Would you say," he spoke slowly, "that unless a man had been taught as a boy he could never learn? I mean when he's middle aged."

"I think it would be very difficult. No doubt it's been done."

He reflected again and threw away his cigarette with a slow deliberate gesture.

"When my mother died about ten years ago my elder brother sent me out some of her things, and among them was a grand piano. I got it tuned and so on. I always keep it tuned. I bought a book which was supposed to enable you to teach yourself. I suppose I started too late. At all events I was never able to learn the most elementary things. I love music and there that thing sits in my house and I can't even play 'God Save the King' on it. I hate the gramophone, it makes my head buzz. Occasionally someone turns up here who can play. By the way do you play fox-trots and jazz and that sort of thing?"

"No."

"Good. What I wanted to ask you was whether you'd come round and play sometime."

"Look here, I am not being modest, but I really do play very badly indeed. Strictly speaking, by any musical standard, I can't play at all."

"Yes, but by normal standards you can play a bit. If you're here tomorrow evening will you come round to my place at about a quarter to eight, for dinner? I hope you will."

I found his predicament so easy to understand and it

was so obvious that my strumming really gave pleasure to his untrained ear that I accepted without more ado.

"That's very good of you," he said, "you're sure it won't bore you?"

"Bore *me*? Good heavens, no."

I took some trouble in the preparation of my after-dinner concert and really my performance was not too bad. I began with a very easy continuo by Handel introducing into this a great many leitmotifs from "The Ring." I then went on to a misuse of Bach, Beethoven, Haydn and Schumann. Sensing that my audience was quite uneducated I played without restraint; and once or twice I became quite deeply moved, as for example by my funeral march of Siegfried into which I introduced *Lohengrin's* swan. I closed with bits of *Parsifal* and the Dresden Amen. Vereker was lying in his chair, his head thrown back. His eyes were narrowed and his mouth set as though keeping down his emotion. I had played for three quarters of an hour. There ensued a long silence.

"Thank you very much," he said. "You must be tired. Have a whisky and soda." And while I was drinking he said: "You know, you're lucky. I'd give a lot to be able to do that."

I could say nothing. I felt base, though I had no need to do so. Had I not warned him against my playing more than once? But all the same I felt base. I cannot pretend, however, that my scruples overcame my delight in the hoax I was so strangely forced to perpetrate on my admirer. That I bowl over, that I reduce to a quivering emotional mass a large and distinguished audience with my playing of a Beethoven Sonata is a not ignoble day-dream to which I own, and Vereker had given me an opportunity to put this unlikely ambition into something resembling action. I enjoyed that. He asked me how long I was staying.

"I am not sure," I answered. "Mrs. Featherstone told me that Mrs. Homer might be back quite soon and I should like to see her. So I shall stay a day or two on the chance."

Vereker twitched his nostrils in a way which suggested he was thinking of something else.

"I see," he said. He then asked me if I was too tired to play more that night. I was touched by this solicitude for the artist, and replied that I should love to play for half an hour more.

During the second part of the concert, the effect on him of my long and monstrous commentary on the masters was to stimulate the thoughts that were in his mind. He sat forward on his chair, holding his hands together not far from his mouth, and looking through his narrowed eyes at the cigarette which he held there. He looked up once and said: "I say, play that part again!" But it was evident that his mind was not now directly on the music, and that rather than it he was enjoying the fluency and ease which music gave to his own ideas. When I had finished, he sat silent, and then he slowly lowered his hands and exhaled smoke with a long sigh. He was still smiling as he paid me in whisky and soda. We had become close friends through our shared love of music, for although the concert had been a fraud, the love which made me play, and made him listen, was genuine. He broke the silence.

"The general told me you came down from Siwandi-stan with that man Bishop."

"Yes."

"Can you remember if you stopped anywhere?"

"Yes. Shabbareg."

"Did Bishop talk to any one there?"

"Only with the petrol man, and with a Pathan who was travelling with us. We sat together at Shabbareg, the three of us, and drank tea."

"This Pathan. Did he leave a gun?"

"Yes."

"You and Bishop talked together most of the time. And sometimes with the Pathan. Did Bishop talk to any one else?"

"Only the chap who sold petrol."

"That's all?"

"Yes. Why do you ask me all these questions?"

Vereker pulled at his cigarette. "Bishop's a funny fel-low," he said, "he's the sort of chap who's crooked by nature. Wherever he's been he's done very well and got the sack."

"There's something depressing about him."

Vereker did not speak for some time and then he said:

"You knew Mrs. Homer, you said. Do you know Homer too?"

"No."

He paused again and then said:

"Don't publish this. They went into Siwandistan to dig for something or other, and they were pinched by brigands. She never goes with him; very annoying that this should happen the only time she does. Well, I've never paid a ransom yet and I won't now, but I must get her out. From what you tell me Bishop seems to be doing his stuff all right."

"Are they in danger? This is terrible."

"No, I don't think so. Oh, no, they're in no danger. Not yet."

"Have you any idea where they are?"

"I'm practically sure they're somewhere near Shabbareg."

"I wish Bishop had told me. I'd have done something to help."

He smiled.

"It's rather a specialized job," he said.

"Yes, I suppose it is. Everything is. All the same I'd like to help. She's a great friend."

"I think you may be able to help. That's why I mentioned this business. If you can, I'll let you know."

"She is still quite lovely, isn't she?"

"Yes, she is. You can drive a car, can't you?"

"Yes."

He lit another cigarette, and then said: "You might help — driving a car."

Mrs. Homer meant very little to me, and never had, but once she had seemed to. When I heard of her capture by brigands I found myself once more in the glow of a fancied passion, but it was not this glow alone which made me so long to join in the rescue. It was that here for the first time I met life in the shape and form of a second-rate novelette, and I wanted to be part of it. We all day-dream in that style; it is one of the most natural, most irrepressible, and one of the silliest activities of the mind.

Good art never comes from daydreaming, but novelettes do, and I am sure that the real reason why they are widely read is that they come from such deep depths in our nature. They are irresistible. And though I was sick of adventure I could not resist this stock piece. I was very young too.

"When did you hear about this?" I asked.

"About five days ago."

"Nearly a week! Is she locked up in a dungeon and that sort of thing?"

"Did you stay with any Siwandis?"

"Yes."

"Was it very unpleasant?"

"It was rather fun."

"Well, she's having great fun too. Very likely they don't realize that they are prisoners. The Siwandis are good chaps in their way."

"Do tell me more about it."

He pulled at his cigarette, and poured out some more whisky. Vereker was like a man acting the part of an Indian senior official in a play. Every gesture was correct, and his phrases were perfectly expectable. I had often met the same thing among the English in India. This was not because they were shallow or theatrical people but because empires are theatrical things. Even the least imaginative were conscious of taking part in a drama.

"It would take a long time to tell you in detail. Roughly this is what happened. There are some gun and opium smugglers in jug here. They come from a Shabbareg tribe. Your friend who left his gun there is one of their liaison officers, so to speak, and he was the fellow who came and saw me about a week ago, and told me that their tribe was in ferment and would rise against us, and invade Jai' unless these opium and gun-runners were liberated. That was not a likely story. I said nothing for a while and so, as always happens, he found he had a few more bits of news. The tribe, I was told, would be satisfied if I paid large compensations to the smugglers' families. When I said that I saw no reason to do so he told me that I underrated the urgency of the matter. Anti-British feeling was running high, so high in fact, that one of the Khans had had to rescue Mr. and Mrs. Homer from the popular fury. If he had not taken them into his house and set a guard at the door they would have been killed. The whole story is bunk from beginning to end, of course, except the very last detail — viz. Mr. and Mrs. Homer. They've been nabbed. Not rescued, nabbed. Well, your friend went back with a message of thanks from me to the anonymous protector of the Homers, and Bishop picked him up again at Mashad Islam. Bishop thinks he has located the Homers, and he has an idea how he can get them out. His idea seems sound enough and he's never let me down on this sort of job, so I'm giving him his head. They'll be back in a few days. If Bishop's dodge fails I'll have to think of something else. They're safe enough. But don't tell anyone." He smiled. "Childish the Siwandis are . . . That chap always goes through the farce of leaving his gun behind. He thinks it creates a wonderful impression on me."

"So you fancy there's no real danger to them?"

He pursed his lips and shook his head.

"Very unlikely."

"And you will really let me know if I can help."

"Of course. Will you play to me again some other night?"

"How about tomorrow?"

"I'll expect you at a quarter to eight."

I went, and when I was alone my thoughts went back to Mrs. Homer.

I had known her as Harriet Rowan and it was still an effort for me to think of her as the bearer of another name, and also to think of her as separated from her sister Georgiana.

I remembered them as two of the most fashionable young unmarried women of the late 'twenties. They were the daughters of a shipping magnate called Sir John Rowan. They went the rounds together, splendidly; they sparkled at every ball in London throughout the different seasons, having always first dined at whatever was the most impressive dinner given for the occasion. In the opera season, there in the best box at Covent Garden sat the two Rowan girls, and they were always to be found at the time of Ascot, Goodwood, or Doncaster races, staying in the greatest of the neighbouring country houses. In August they moved to the north for the grouse and stag business, and south again for the St. Leger. They hunted, but only in the shires. In one respect alone they did not follow the routine. They never left England; they never went to Venice or the South of France, and this was by the wish of their rarely seen parents who disapproved of the laxity of foreign pleasure resorts. They were more respectably bourgeois than most of their friends; more careful.

Harriet was the lovelier of those two lovely sisters. She was better dressed, too, wearing clothes made in a severely modest style which set off her looks finely. She was certainly then the most beautiful girl I had even seen. There was a smoothness about her skin which was extraordinary, the pores must have been minute, and if marble were not a weary word of praise, I would say that her skin was like marble. Her eyes were deep blue, and over them she had a little perpendicular forehead. She was a light brunette. I can feel again the thrill of seeing her walk into a room, with the blank expression on her face giving her a wonderful last touch of innocent mystery.

She was quite dumb; she could talk about nothing at all, nor did she try. It was usual to complain about this, and people often said: "Oh, Harriet's so dumb, so deadly dumb." But between all young men who knew her there was a deep deep understanding that we would, at a favourable sign, give up all for the blockhead. People used to say that she was sexless and hard and a ruthless go-getter, but the malicious talk against her was largely made up of sour-grape grumbling. Her power over men was far greater than that normally exerted by girlish beauty. Distinguished people of mature years were liable to become transparent exhibitionists in her presence. Her nicest trait was her love for her sister and the good humour with which she took her occasional teasing.

Georgiana Rowan, whom we used to call "Georgie," was very different from Harriet. Her beauty was of a more obvious open kind, and her charm more ordinary. She had golden hair, and her complexion was a matter of roses and milk and orchards and that sort of thing. She was of larger build, though she had the same elegance of action as her sister, and she was expressive. She had wit of a kind and sometimes, out of fun, I think, though there may have been more in it, she used to chill off Harriet's admirers. I may give too strong an idea of the difference between them. With all their contrasts they were very much of a pair. They used to look charming, like two gazelles, when they arrived anywhere together, and they were forever arriving. It was generally understood that Harriet would marry a millionaire duke, and Georgie an earl with an income. One of the things that put Georgie's destiny a little lower than her sister's was that she was too ubiquitous, not rare enough, too anxious for everyone to enjoy her golden hair and roses. She did not, like Harriet, confine herself to a little fashionable world. She often bounced off her pedestal in search of adventure; she used to go to parties in Chelsea and Bloomsbury, as a result of which excursions there arose among their more usual companions the familiar and resented phenomenon of "one of Georgie's extraordinary friends."

Well, as the reader must have guessed, fate played a great prank on the Rowan girls. Georgie married her earl with an income all right, but before that Harriet had married one of Georgie's extraordinary friends. I need not explain that he was an archaeologist called Homer. Georgie — how angry her parents must have been with her afterwards — used to meet him in London. He would never have met Harriet if Georgie had not asked him to

stay with her family in the country. That did the trick.
After a very short time indeed the nice unassuming fellow was engaged to the silent beauty. There was a great
wedding which covered up any sense of disappointment.
The "whole of London" and Harriet's native Cheshire
were invited. The ceremony took place in St. Margaret's,
Westminster; some Duchess or other lent her huge house
for the reception, and at the top of the vast ugly marble
stairs Sir John and Lady Rowan, whom hardly any of
their noble guests had ever seen or thought of before,
stood like a couple of rubicund pumps. I was among
those who pumped them, went on and pumped a grey
woman in a purple cloud (some Homeric aunt or other),
and then, with what was a little hidden orgy of self-pity,
I squeezed Harriet's fingers, and then took the hand of
unknown Homer. I then turned to the not large labour
of quenching my grief in champagne. Without hope of
any kind I had loved her in my fashion, a very futile one
I guess. Now, I felt the passion shedding away from me.
In this, though I did not know it, I was in some way following the mass. As the last photographers walked away
from the honeymoon train, the Homers were left with
their lonely life. Public interest in beautiful Harriet
walked away too.

All this had happened six years before.

To tell the truth I had almost forgotten her myself. I
had seen Georgie, Lady Desmaney as she was now, before I left for the East and she had told me that Harriet
now lived in Jaideri where she had been for three years,
and that before Jaideri she had lived in Ceylon. I put her
name against Jaideri in my address book. When I found

that she was not there the emotion of disappointment which I experienced was very slight, and though I stayed in the hope of seeing her again, I must confess that I might not have done this if I had not found it enjoyable to to stay on doing nothing. I do not wish to display some wonderful hardness in my nature, but rather to indicate that my affection for Harriet was built upon weak foundations: that the blaze of my passion, which was still my light in that direction, had grown quickly dim as happens to counterfeit fire, and that when I sought for the stuff of a warm friendship I found only lumber and painted flames and idle gas jets which looked melancholy in a shaft of sunlight. When I heard of her danger, however, I found myself pulling out those properties again, and fixing up the floats and straws and footlights, and the whole stage, in so far as I could do with such old rickety machinery, for a grand performance of Saint George, the Dragon, and the Maid. I should like to have supported the main role, but Bishop had already been cast for that.

I did not keep my second appointment to play to Vereker because by then the action of the drama in which I had been caught had fairly started. On the morning of the day following my piano recital Vereker rang me up in order first to be assured that my promise to help had been on no since-regretted impulse. Assured, he said to me: "I am still relying on your absolute discretion. Not a word to any one. Go to Bishop at the Macready garage and he'll tell you what to do. Thanks."

I made my way through the packed clamorous streets to one of the main thoroughfares of the inner town and there I picked out the name of Macready written in large letters over the arch of a wide gateway. Noise, omnipresent in the streets, was concentrated here, for there was a great crowd of Indians gathered in groups, arguing, with what looked like fierce hatred, over the prices of seats, for Macready's ran bus services in this province. I shouldered my way through the crowd and after a little while found Bishop leaning against the bonnet of a car smoking a cigarette and reading a tattered order-book. In European clothes he looked much more of an outcast than he had done in his turban and hanging-out shirt. He had on the threadbare dress of happier times. His hat was not a working hat. It was a slightly old-fashioned trilby with a bound brim, worn into a state of filthy comfort.

"Oh, hallo!" he cried and spat out his cigarette. "What d'you want to buy a lorry for?" He winked with a rapidity which made that suspicious sign safe. Only half understanding I said nothing. At that moment an Indian clerk came up. Bishop went on:

"For the sort of job you're in, a Chev's the answer. I've got a nice Chev. Like to see it?"

"Yes," I said.

I presumed that the masquerade had to be kept up owing to the continued presence of the clerk, a glistening man in pale pink tweeds, who came with us towards a lorry.

"Lots of life in 'er yet," went on Bishop kicking a tire. "Suit you nicely."

I searched in my mind for the obvious next remark. I found it.

"Can I try it sometime?"

Bishop looked at the car, looked at the clerk, looked at me, looked down. "Can I try it! Did you think we were a bloody great shop in Piccadilly? That's the difficulty with you rich blighters. Think I've nothing to do but sell you second-hand cars and save twopence 'alfpenny on deterioration. Christ! What d'you think I keep cars for? To take people like you for rides in them in case you might want to buy them?" He droned on for a long time in this strain. I was completely lost. I presumed that he wished the clerk and any other stray listener to mistake me for a prospective purchaser — but why this long harangue against me? I remember wondering how much was part of the necessary play-acting and how much he was taking an opportunity to express his discomfort in the world.

"Well, what d'you suggest?" I asked.

"That you give me a hundred down and take it out of the garage."

"But I *must* try it out," I exclaimed. Surely I was not supposed to be a lunatic?

"Must you? Well . . ." The clerk's attention was drawn to two little boys who were committing some mischief on the number plate. He darted at them and then back again to us but not before Bishop had been able to say: "Start at six-thirty. Shabbareg. To-night."

"I don't care where I go," I said, "though preferably where there's a hill, and I am in no hurry. You know who I am buying it for?" I ended, pleading with him to let me know.

61

"*I* don't know," he answered rudely. "Some rich b—r in Bombay isn't it?"

I laughed. "That's right. He wants it before next month. And I've got to try it."

I began to like the little boys for they had returned to their ministrations at the back of the car, and the clerk was again absent for a while. Not changing his expression nor his attitude, Bishop remained leaning against the car, jingling money in his pockets. He said:

"You start from here at six-thirty taking a quarter-ton Diesel engine to Shabbareg. I'm going on ahead to survey, starting in about half an hour. Take it to that garage in Shabbareg and sleep with it. There's a chap going up with you. Don't let on to him. You're quite all right. Day after tomorrow a lorry'll come down across country from a lad called Sher Ali Khan. Pretend you expect it tomorrow. It's a big Ford. Make sure it's his. Sher Ali Khan. See that the engine is loaded on it. Send it off. Don't go with it. See that everything's loaded properly. Don't break anything for God's sake. Got all that clear? Get some mud in the carburettor. Bust the engine of the car up, but so it'll go together again, and wait for me. I'll try and get to you by — what's today? Monday — well, by Friday night. Look out — here he is again. So you'd know," Bishop raised his voice slightly "how to load up a Diesel. You're a bit of an engineer. Well, well, you rich sods aren't all such cissies. But you can't rough it."

"Oh yes. Certainly."

"Not like I'd like you to if you was to try out my car

62

so that I'd lose no money. You're a bit too rich and soft for that."

"As I'm not a millionaire your insults don't worry me particularly. What d'you want me to do with this car of yours?" Then for the benefit of the clerk he put to me the proposition which I had already heard. I accepted. The clerk interrupted several times to assure me of the barbarous horror of the garage at Shabbareg.

"It'll be an adventure. I shall enjoy it."

"I'm sorry if I was a bit rude," said Bishop. "I thought perhaps you was a slug but you aren't a slug at all."

"That's the nicest thing anyone's ever said to me," I answered.

The noise in the garage, of yelling, of engines, of vendors, was oppressive; cheerlessly, pointlessly violent. The sun was burning my head through my hat.

"Well, you be here at six o'clock," said Bishop.

"All right."

The Indian clerk was gazing at me and I wondered why, and then it occurred to me that probably here in India as elsewhere in the East, everything which takes place is a mask for something else behind it; that perhaps the clerk suspected an intrigue, and Bishop's extraordinary behaviour had not taken him in. I remember that at the same time a suspicion entered my head that stern men impervious to rudeness are often actors who are enjoying themselves.

Bishop, as I have said, had been cast for the principal role and I was a scene-shifter. While I hoped for a brief appearance as the squire of the saint, my main task was confined to gallant discomfort suffered in secret, and I will not describe my experiences in detail.

At six-thirty that evening I appeared at Macready's garage where I found the Chevrolet lorry loaded with big contorted shapes, all packed in sacking, and the promised "chap" awaiting me. He was an Indian, young, robust, and rather handsome; he was merrier than most of his compatriots, talked English of a kind and a little Afghan Persian, and when he wound up the car, or leaped up to tend the iron load, or merely drove, he seemed as though he were engaged in a ballet on the subject of his trade. He swung himself hither and thither like a trapeze artist.

We took the wheel in turns, passed the frontier with no difficulty as my visa was still valid, and reached Shabbareg at about eleven o'clock at night. Following Bishop's instructions I made myself a nest at the end of the truck, and slept with the engine. The next day was Tuesday and nothing happened material to this story. Following the plan I began to complain about the delay of the lorry. Wednesday morning, I remember, was spent with a book on a bench amid the chatter of the coffee-house and the sufferings of constipation. I met only one man, a fat elderly one, who could talk to me (he knew a little Persian), and he was a bore unfortunately. I complained to him about the delay of the lorry. I only read about twenty pages for I had to glance up whenever I heard the sound of a lorry arriving, and there were many, and in so doing I invariably lost my place. After lunch I fell asleep and awoke at four to see the "chap," and others, loading our cargo on to a big Ford lorry which was encrusted with the white dust of North East India. I came forward to make sure whether or not this was the lorry of Sher Ali which had come from inland. It was. At half-past five it was driven off, smoothly for a hundred yards or so, and then bump onto a stone-strewn country track. Even at our distance we could hear some clanking. I hoped all was well. I then turned to my next job, namely, the destruction of the engine of the car. I told the chap that I would drive up the hill by myself in order to look for an antelope. He insisted on coming too. I failed to prevent him and as soon as I was seen to climb into the driver's seat and start up the engine, there was a rush of Pathans from the coffee-house, and in a few seconds some fifteen of them were sitting in the truck and two more in front. When I attempted to address them they all shouted: "Mashad Islam" and cheered. My Persian-speaking bore was among them. I told him that I was only going to the top of the hill to look for an antelope, and asked that he and his friends would kindly get out. But a ride was quite as enjoyable as a free lift to Mashad Islam. My words were translated and the barbarians banged their rifle butts on the floor of the truck, greeting my announcement with horrid applause. There was nothing to be done so I smiled and shrugged my shoulders and drove them up the hill wondering how in the world I could smash up the engine without their noticing. But in fact I experienced no difficulty for they smashed it for me.

About four miles from Shabbareg, I made the engine seem unwell, by driving with the choke full out. Soon it stalled, and I shook my head. "Something wrong," I said.

I stopped, and, howling with delight, the Pathans leaped to the ground. I explained, via the chap and the bore, that here was the place, but that I must attend to the engine. I thought that they would separate and go stalking; I had overlooked the fact that the appeal of antelopes to them was almost nothing compared to that of a piece of modern machinery. They stayed, enthralled. "It's the carburettor," I muttered as I opened the bonnet. They pressed round and each one thrust in a hand with roars of delight like children round a bran tub. It needed no great ingenuity to direct their fingers to the coil, having previously pocketed the spare ones while pretending to wipe my hands in the grass. I filled my mouth with mud, and then spat it into the carburettor, pretending to blow it clean. I climbed back into the driver's seat and started up the engine, which now gave signs of authentic illness. We bowled freely down the hill and the Pathans had to push me the last mile home.

The next two days were passed in cleaning the carburettor, very slowly, and looking for a coil. By Friday night the car was mended but Bishop did not arrive. I broke the coil once more, pretending that this new one was defective. I found another on Saturday, mended the car, but there was still no sign of Bishop. He was a day late. This made my part in the plan difficult, as there was now no excuse for my remaining. My movements were followed with interest and I could not get away with another defective coil. I was wondering how to break the car again without causing suspicion. I began to fear for Bishop and Harriet. In the light of my anxiety every face began to take on a look of awful ferocity. My Pathan friends, with whom I kept up acquaintance with growls and grins, seemed to my eyes to grow sinister by gradual degrees. As my self-confidence weakened, their hostility mysteriously increased. By midnight Bishop had not arrived. I was the only person, except the armed watchman, still awake, and I sat by my smoking lamp reading my book, glancing up, and losing my place. Suddenly, at about one, I was overcome with fatigue and after laying my mattress on one of the wooden trestles in the coffee-house porch (for I no longer needed to guard the contents of the truck), I fell into a deep sleep.

I awoke suddenly and gazed horror-struck at a figure bending over me. A cold morning breeze touched my cheek and I saw that I had been awakened by Bishop, in Pathan clothes once more, who was holding my shoulder and looking down. So Bishop was back. Stars were still shining but on the horizon was the sign of dawn. I said:

"Hullo, Bishop. Everything all right?"

"Yes. Is the car mended?"

"Yes."

"Then let's go."

"I must pay."

"I've paid for you. I said you'd told me to."

"Very well, let's go."

The watchman was gazing at us miserably. The noise of the starting engine smote the silence with its sudden ugliness. I climbed into the front seat and sat with Bishop and the chap, and without a word in that dead hour we

67

drove away from Shabbareg. Where was Harriet? Bishop had said nothing about her, and I guessed that he did not want to talk in front of the chap.

I slept a little and when I awoke Bishop was talking to the man at the frontier. After a very short delay we drove on. Bishop looked exhausted; his face seemed redder, and his eyes were unnaturally wide open and expressionless.

"Let me drive for a bit."

"No. I'll just go on. If I stopped I'd fall asleep and I've got some things to do yet."

"I see."

The chap's head was on my shoulder and he was sleeping like a child. The mountains were now fast returning to the full emphasis of day and their summits showed the first stages of strong shadows and glow. I began to awake. I said to Bishop: "Where's Mrs. Homer?"

He raised his eyebrows and said tonelessly: "She's all right." He gave a little smiling twitch to his mouth which I took to mean that the rescue had been successful. He said no more, and I asked no more. We approached Jaideri and I began to fall back into my interrupted sleep painfully. As my head fell forward with a wrench to my neck, or back and sideways, I was aware through the jungle of sleep that we were not entering the town but driving round the outskirts and that we turned away from it up into a little used lane. We stopped and Bishop got out. I fell forward on the dashboard and returned farther into my agonizing sleep in the dreams of which I heard noises in the truck behind me. I was not sure whether I saw a figure wrapped in a rug walking up a garden path to a door held open by a servant, or whether I dreamed this also, until, as Bishop climbed back into the driver's seat, I asked him: "Who was that in a rug?"

And he answered: "Mrs. Homer."

She had been asleep, lying in the back. The next stop was at my hotel. I had a bath and then slept deeply in my bed.

When I awoke it was dark again. I wondered whether it was Sunday night or Monday morning, and lay in bed half awake, wondering for a time. The problem was solved by a hotel servant who came into the room and told me that it was seven o'clock, and he added that Mr. Beesoof was downstairs asking for me. I got out of bed and put on a dressing-gown and asked for him to be sent up.

When Bishop came into the room I noticed a change in his appearance. (He was one of those men with whose appearance it was difficult to become familiar.) He looked preternaturally clean and his coarse ill-cut hair had been plastered down on his head in the manner of a schoolboy's on Prize Giving Day. He had on his worn-out suit but an obviously clean shirt and collar. He walked into the room with his bravado rolling gait and with his hands in his pockets, stopping to kick the door to with his heel.

"Hullo," he said. "How are you feeling?"

"Much worse. I've been to sleep."

"I've had some sleep too. I needed it, I can tell you."

"I bet you did. Sit down and let's have some beer."

"D'you mind if I have a whisky?" He opened the door

and yelled: "Boy!" and then, in his fluent Hindustani, he ordered drinks.

"This isn't much of a hotel," he said looking round the walls with his sad eyes. "Clean, I suppose. Do you know Shepheard's in Cairo?"

"Yes."

"That's a great hotel."

There was a pause while our drinks were brought in and served to us. We were both suffering from that heaviness of spirit which oppresses people who have just enjoyed a too well earned sleep, and so our conversation seemed forced. We toasted each other and drank, grimly. I was the first to speak.

"How are the Homers?"

"They're all right. Mrs. Homer's back in her house. We're fetching Homer from Shabbareg tomorrow."

"Shabbareg? He's there still?"

"Yes." He made an effort to explain. "He stayed behind. As a sort of hostage. We'll fetch him tomorrow. Vereker doesn't want you to come this time — it'd look funny. So Ahmed an' I'll go up."

"Right. And now I want you to tell me what it was all about."

"Don't you know?"

"Only half. I know that the Homers were kidnapped and that you got them out — but I don't know how. What was I doing driving that cargo of iron up to Shabbareg and busting up the engine of your car?"

"Why it was all part of my scheme."

"What was your scheme?"

He then started to tell me of the ingenious device by

which he had lured the captor into surrender of his
victims, but he told the story so badly, wandering into
digressions at every turn, that I will not attempt to
reproduce his words. He spoilt his tale by what I can
best describe as a kind of tedious and self-commiserating
boastfulness. But the facts were interesting and these I
will give concisely.

About thirty-five miles from Shabbareg there dwelt
two landowners, Sher Ali Khan and Sultan Mahmud,
their lands adjoining and their castles separated by a
"robat" or stage, which means by eight miles or so. They
were brigands and mutual enemies. Their lands lay not
far from a range of mountains whence they got their
water. In both their lands the water was collected into
cisterns and pumped, for which purpose they both maintained between twenty and twenty-five pumps worked
by camels, mules and oxen. Sultan Mahmud had learned
that one Diesel engine could work all his pumps, saving
him from the need of maintaining his many beasts. About
a year previously he had made inquiries of Bishop as to
the cost of these contrivances, and the possibility of ob-
taining one. His desire was not only aroused because of
the practical advantages of a mechanical pump, but also
by the fact that his possession of one would impress his
neighbours. Bishop, however, was a bargainer: he would
only propose extortionate terms, and he suggested that
the sale of Diesel engines was controlled by the Government of India, which was not true in those days. He
wished to bring every circumstance of dread to the assistance of his bargain. In the course of time Sher Ali Khan
heard of the Sultan's negotiations and he was moved with

jealousy. On several occasions he told Bishop that it would be a dreadful thing for the Government of India if they sold a Diesel engine to the Sultan. They would never be respected again, he said.

Bishop remembered all this when he heard that Sher Ali Khan was the kidnapper of Mr. and Mrs. Homer.

On the same day as I arrived at Shabbareg, Bishop made his way by car on a rough road, to a little caravan-serai about four miles from our coffee-house which was kept by a transport contractor. From here he hired a mule and rode off in the direction of Sultan Mahmud's land. He slept about twenty miles from Shabbareg and on Tuesday morning he came into the neighbourhood of Sher Ali Khan. He took care to ride within view of the castle. He was seen, and some horsemen were sent galloping out to make inquiries of the solitary rider. They recognized him of course (every one between Mashad Islam and Jaideri knew Beesoof) and they begged him to come indoors to see his old friend. He hesitated and in his excuses let slip the secret: he was travelling on business to Sultan Mahmud. They told him that the two lords were at peace and when they asked again if he would come with them to Sher Ali he accepted.

The Khan received him with enthusiastic affection and insisted that he should interrupt his journey and spend the night with them. He took a great deal of persuasion but at last, as though reluctantly, accepted. When he was alone he wanted to make quite sure that the Homers were indeed in the castle. He went into the courtyard and whistled "Tipperary" loudly, and then strained his ears. Sure enough he heard a distant voice,

unmistakably English. It was probably saying: "Good
Lord, there's a fellow knows 'Tipperary.'" Over lunch
the Khan attempted every device to discover the nature
of Bishop's business with Sultan Mahmud, and at last his
guest appeared to fall into a trap and confessed: he was
going to survey on the Sultan's land for the installation
of a Diesel engine. When his host asked why the Government of India pandered to such a rogue Bishop answered by telling him of the circumstances: Sultan
Mahmud had promised to obtain the release of two English people who were being held prisoner on the excuse
of protection by someone in his neighbourhood. There
then followed a long intricate comedy in which the Khan
warned Bishop that he was being deceived, and slowly
seemed to persuade him that he was approaching the
wrong man. In the evening the Khan swore to Bishop on
an oath that he would risk his life in order to rescue the
two English people if, instead of installing the Diesel engine in Sultan Mahmud's land, he would install it in his.
He would pay a splendid price. They argued long into
the night. In the morning Bishop consented, and it was
decided that the lorry should set off next day. (It was
away for some reason not important to this story).

The same morning Bishop surveyed. Next day, towards midday, soon after the lorry had left, the Khan
sought him out. Sher Ali presented the appearance of
having just returned from a long ride. Difficulties had
arisen. The anonymous captor would liberate the woman
but not the man. Why? The Khan cast up his eyes and
beat his breast: ah, this man was a hard man and he, the
Khan, out of his love for Bishop, had paid him a great

sum in order to rescue these unfortunate prisoners, but the captor was not yet wholly appeased. Could not Bishop perhaps help him by giving some money towards the ransom, then perhaps he could rescue both. Bishop answered that the Government of India never paid a ransom. They did not, however, mind selling a Diesel engine at cost price to a liberator. He could deduct £150 from what the Khan owed. So far as Bishop was concerned he could only act on those terms. He had surveyed, the engine was coming up, the Khan's nephew, who had been educated at Calcutta, knew how to install it. Certain essential parts, as his nephew would agree when he saw the engine, needed to be sent up from Jaideri. Bishop would deliver these in return for the man, having first conducted the woman safely to her home. He was sorry to treat the Khan so, but he was acting for a Government renowned for its harshness.

I gathered from Bishop's account of the matter that they argued over this until Thursday evening by which time the pump had arrived, and the Khan's educated nephew had thoroughly examined it. At last with tears and wails, declaring that for the sake of his people he must obtain a Diesel engine, even if this ruined him, Sher Ali consented to carry the full burden of the ransom. At dawn on Friday morning, Bishop met Mrs. Homer. She was conducted to a place where he was waiting outside the castle, and she was provided with swift horses, and a couple of grooms because, for the sake of secrecy, the Khan did not wish to convey her in his little touring car, though this would have befitted her rank. The rest I knew. Bishop would take up the spare parts, in return for which he would receive Homer, on Monday. That was the story.

Bishop asked for some more whisky. While he was pouring it out I said: "It took you a very long time getting back. I suppose she was tired, and the horses were slow?"

"Yes, that's right."

"It was waiting for you yesterday that got me down. I thought you'd had an accident."

"Oh, no, we were all right."

"I used to know Mrs. Homer well. It's a long time since I've seen her. Is she still very good looking?"

Bishop gulped at his whisky and said: "Good looking? H'm. So so. I didn't really notice. Not bad, I suppose."

"It was your first meeting?" I asked, rather surprised.

"Yes. I see no one here. I'm not popular."

This intimate confession embarrassed me. I feebly replied: "I'm sure you're wrong."

"Oh, am I? The only English people I could mix with here are Tommies, and they don't want me."

There were a hundred possible polite answers to this but on the other hand what Bishop had just told me was obviously true. I said nothing and we both drank. In the silence that followed I thought over the story he had told me.

"There's one thing in your tale which I don't quite follow. Sher Ali told you that the Homers were being held captive by someone else and that he was only the go-between. But surely he knew that Mrs. Homer would tell you the truth."

Bishop was leaning over his drink, still gloomy over

75

what he had said before. He looked up stupidly and sighed, and then, as though collecting himself with an effort, he said:

"The danger was the other way round — that I would tell Mrs. Homer. But old Sher Ali knows the form all right. He's often been to Jai' and met English people. Pathans get on well with the English people here. Not like the Indians."

"You mean — "

"Oh, she'd no idea that they were captives. They'd been told that someone else wanted to kidnap them. I expect they felt damned grateful to Sher Ali."

"Yes. But Sher Ali did not want you to know that they had been in his castle all the time?"

Bishop raised his eyebrows and depressed his mouth at the corners: "No, that's true," he said, "something in that." And then he looked down at his drink again and the gloomy smile spread over his roguish face: "But he'd nothing to worry about. Who am I? Mrs. Homer's not going to waste much time talking to a fellow like me. Oh, Lord no. She's one sort and I'm another. She's got position. That's what you've got to have in India. Sher Ali knows all about that. In a way she's got more in common with him. She'd believe him sooner than me. I'm just a lousy confidence trickster — that's all. An outsider. Nothing."

It appeared to me that Bishop was now exaggerating the situation a great deal, but the very fact that he could do so excited my resentment. I felt angry at the thought of that priggish girl: I saw her suddenly vividly in my mind, with her dumb insensitive respectability; and I felt some of my exasperation directed at Bishop too: he was taking his humiliation with such spiritless abjection. Why couldn't he stand up for himself? I expressed something of what I felt.

"Well, I've not much sympathy for you," I said awkwardly. Bishop gave a violent start. "If you ride forth and rescue a lovely woman and can't make her respect you for it, the fault is your own."

"What d'you mean?" he said with wide eyes and a very serious expression.

"Just what I say. If I'd had your job, Mrs. Homer would be gaping at me with wonder and awe. I'd tell her; I'd make it plain that she owed her life to me. If she failed to pay me the honours due to a hero I would certainly not take it lying down. But you do, and that's why I've no sympathy. It makes me angry with you."

He was looking down and he slowly shook his head, smiling and sighing again: "Oh, it's easy to talk like that. You don't know me, and you don't know India. I'm a washout. Mrs. Homer's a regular mem-sahib. I say nothing against her. It's India. It's the way I live. I'm different."

"I think that's ridiculous. People are different everywhere, and lead lives different from each other. If people behave offensively in India it's because they are offensive people. It's nothing to do with India."

"Come and live here and see. After two years we wouldn't meet like this and drink and chat together. I wouldn't call on you. It'd be no use. You'd be a sahib, and I'd just be 'that filthy Bishop.' I've seen it happen."

"Oh? And what do *you* do about it? You've got into

77

the habit of thinking along those lines and you force
people to act back. You forget that I used to know Mrs.
Homer very well, and she has a charming nature."

"I say nothing against her. She probably has got a
'charming nature' or whatever you call it."

"Well then . . ."

He drank and shook his head again and sighed: "Oh,
it doesn't make *me* have a 'charming nature.' I've been
helped out hundreds of times but I always sink back. I'm
not the kind who floats. Vereker's been good to me but
only because he needs someone like me who can pull off
a dirty deal whenever he wants it done. I'm the thief
who he sets to catch a lot of other thieves. That's all I'm
good for."

I believed what he had told me.

"You exaggerate," I answered insincerely.

From what Vereker and he himself had said I could
believe that Bishop's past had been punctuated with incidents distressing to his compatriots in India, and to their
great predilection for decency of a certain kind. In-
civility, lawlessness, and the smart profiteering of the
rich they could forgive, but not the kind of small swind-
ling which I guessed was the main current of Bishop's
daily business. It was shameful because it was not done
on the big Western scale. It was not impressive. It was
quite rightly described as descending to a lower level. I
saw this strange Anglo-Indian life from the outside and
so was not sure about the rights and wrongs of its
conventions, or whether they were needful or merely
foolish. Of one thing only I felt very certain: no con-

siderations of any sort could excuse Harriet Homer's in-
gratitude to Bishop.

"I expect you exaggerate," I said, "because Mrs.
Homer has not . . . how shall I say . . . well — has
not seemed very grateful. Remember I know her well.
She is very shy and tongue-tied."

A forced hollow laugh came from Bishop. "Oh the
hell she is. Every one's a bit tongue-tied when they see
me."

"I give up. You're hopeless."

Harriet had changed very little. Her eyes, her lovely
brown hair with the golden lights, her smooth forehead,
were all much as I remembered them from six years before. She had hardly aged; there was no trace in her
complexion of the Indian sun. I met her two days after
my return, on the evening of Homer's restoration, for
this part of the novelette went through according to plan.
I had rung her up and been invited to dinner. She had
asked me to come early so that we might have a few
minutes chat before the other guests, namely the Featherstones and the greyhound aide, arrived.

"I am so glad to see you," she said, holding out her
hand, "it's such a long time. How are your family?"

I guessed that with her beauty she had preserved most,
if not all, of her dumbness.

"They're very well," I said. "But tell me about
yourself, that's much more exciting. Did Vereker not
tell you that I played an essential and brilliant part in
your rescue?"

79

"Oh, I heard that you drove the lorry down from Shabbareg. That was very kind of you. Why didn't you say something to me at the time?"

"For the good reason that I didn't know you were there. Bishop had to be discreet in front of our driver, so he didn't tell me."

A servant came in with cocktails, and as she took hers she said: "How silly of him." Something in the way she said it revived all my suspicions about her callous treatment of Bishop. She spoke as she might have done of a quite indifferent person whose face she had never troubled to look at.

"I like Bishop," I said.

She replied, "Yes." If I had said, "I like your coal scuttle. It must be useful," her tone would have been quite appropriate to her answer.

Homer came into the room at this moment. I had only seen him once before, on his wedding day, and I only remembered an impression of abnormal tallness, a high forehead, ginger hair, and bulging eyes. The tallness was less striking now that he had grown fatter; the forehead was even higher than aforetime; the fact that his receding hair was long and ill-brushed made me realize that when I had seen him before he had been specially groomed. He looked, at first sight, as though he were a supercilious conceited man, but you could discover in a moment that this was a false impression, and that beneath his exaggeratedly disdainful manner, which was a private comedy he kept up, his nature was warm-hearted. He looked like a portrait of the Tsar Alexander I.

"How very nice to meet you," he said. "Vereker told

me you drove Harriet down from Shabbareg when we were stranded. That was most kind. Thank you very much. Give him a cocktail, sweetie. Well, ring for another. Give me one, too. Really, it was most kind of you. Thanks very much indeed."

"I did very little. Bishop did all the work."

"Bishop? Oh, yes, Bishop."

"He did the rescue work. Without him you might have been in a bad spot, so I gathered from Vereker."

"Vereker was very good about it. He's a very able man, a distinct cut above some other I.C.S. fellows I've had to do with. He knows that Siwandistan country extraordinary well. I have to go there a good deal, and those Khans are an awful lot to do business with. Perfectly preposterous. Someone or other was angling for *ransom* money, or I am much mistaken. *I* can't afford to pay *ransom* money."

He spoke petulantly as if he had been overcharged for something he had bought.

I looked from him to her. She was putting some sewing away in a bag. No one seemed to be playing out the novelette as it deserved except myself, and I had so slight a part that I was hardly worth mentioning in the blurb. I wanted to assert Bishop's heroic claims, but I did not see how I could do so in the presence of this persistent prosiness.

"Do you often go to Siwandistan?"

"Only when I have to. I've done all my digging there for this year and I'm glad, because it's a dreadful country. It's still run on brigand lines you know, and I can't afford the escorts. Then if you don't hire an escort you get into a mess like we did. It's a nuisance. I lost nearly two week's work in that place, hanging about doing nothing. It's preposterous. Let's have another cocktail, sweetie."

The Featherstones arrived. Every one was in evening dress except myself.

"Oh, you should have kept my husband's dinner jacket," said Mrs. Featherstone, "he would have been only too glad."

"I'm leaving tomorrow morning so I sent it back. Thanks all the same."

I sat next to Harriet and our conversation stumbled on with great difficulty. Her pre-marriage fashionable life was too far off to give us a ready subject, and she had nothing to say to me about India. She did not seem to have noticed it. I asked about her husband's archaeological work, and she told me it was very interesting. I asked what she thought of Siwandistan. She said she had gone there because it was cool. I asked her whether Georgie was coming out to visit her, and she said she hoped so, but the journey was very long. I told her she looked perfectly lovely, and she smiled, but even this compliment, which was sincerely offered, failed to enliven our talk. She had nothing to say about it. She was still the most physically desirable woman I had ever seen. She might make a wonderful mistress, I thought, but otherwise this ethereal being was too heavy on the hands to be an enjoyable companion.

After dinner the men sat over the port. Homer was a pleasantly sociable man. Because he was an archaeologist, and therefore an intellectual, he appeared to be a bit of a freak to the General and his aide, but a worthy respectable freak. On his side Homer seemed to be satisfied with this situation. He treated the General with a comic familiarity which was accepted by Featherstone as a queer compliment. These sort of relationships are usually unpleasant, being disfigured by concealed sycophancy, contempt, and humiliation. In the case of these two there was only just enough sympathy between them to make it respectable.

Our drama was touched on shortly before we left the dining-room.

"I hear you had some bother up-country," said the General, "and this fellow," pointing to me, "was sent out to save you."

Homer turned to me with a friendly laugh. "Yes, he drove Harriet down," he said, "and I came this morning. We were held up for over a week before Vereker could arrange the passage."

"He told me something about it. That fellow, what's he called, Sher Ali, who played polo with us in the spring."

"It was Sher Ali who warned us, so we stayed with him. I'd have taken no notice if I'd been alone, but little Harriet wanted to come, so there we were. I ought to have taken an escort from the South, but I just couldn't afford it. I was a B.F. to let Harriet come. It was rotten luck on her, poor mite." He made so little attempt to conceal his deep love for her that the soulful way he uttered her name was slightly embarrassing to strangers.

"Why couldn't Sher Ali see you down to the road?"

"Not his country, old bird. You know the way the

brigand system works? — Good Lord, you're uneducated. It's like this. Your escorts are usually formed of
brigands, or brigand-dealers; middlemen, you know; and
they pay a dividend to the brigands in return for your
safe passage. The point is that your escort must be thoroughly well in with the brigands, or else — well, they just
can't escort you, or themselves for that matter. Sher Ali
was at enmity with the chaps between him and Shabbareg, so until someone came we were stuck. And
then Vereker sent his gallant fellow and we were un-
stuck."

"Bishop did all the work," I said.

"But how could Vereker get through with so little
difficulty?" asked the General. "He never asked me for
help."

Homer shook his head. "He's got them all wonderfully taped. He doesn't forget the important moral of
that game. Unlike old Sher Ali, he always keeps on
speaking terms with outlaws."

We laughed heartily and rose from the table.

Unless Vereker had misled me, which seemed unlikely,
it was evident that the Homers did not fully understand
what had happened to them. This might lessen, but it
could not excuse, Harriet's offence. It was possible, I
supposed, that Vereker wished them to remain in ignorance, so I said nothing about it to her or Homer.

After dinner four of us played bridge, while Homer
and Mrs. Featherstone played piquet. At the end of the
evening I said good-bye because I was leaving by train
early the next morning. I wondered whether to kiss
Harriet, but she chastely and correctly held out her hand,

and in such a way that I imagined that the mildest and most permissible intimacy would strike her as improper. I drove to my hotel with the Featherstones.

As I lay in bed smoking a final cigarette I began to think more kindly of Harriet. She had few brains, and very little character. To expect her to take a bold, different line in India whenever its conventions were unjust, was obviously expecting too much of her; it was unfair; and to blame her was like the contemptible fault of despising people because they do not happen to be clever. There must be something very wrong about Bishop. The way no one would talk about him was queer. It could not be due to snobbishness alone; no one in his right mind is such a snob that he refuses to mention the name of a rescuer because he drops a few aitches and works in a garage. There must be something else, something repulsive about him, which sincerely horrified them all. Yet no matter what that was, and in spite of making allowances for her dumbness, it seemed a pity that Harriet had not enough good feeling to make her say something nice about him, and to prevent her joining in a conspiracy to pretend that her rescue was done by someone else. Poor Harriet, she had the most pitiful lack of personality of anyone I knew. Surrounded by fashion in London this lovely creature had seemed a distinct and definite being, but in the harsh, matter-of-fact, ungraceful life of British India there could be no delusion about her.

Thus I argued to myself. I was right about one or two details. In the main I was wrong. A week afterwards I left India.

Nearly two years later I read in the paper that the Duke of Middlesborough had married Harriet, eldest daughter of Sir John and the late Lady Rowan. Public interest, which had walked away from her first honeymoon train with the cameramen, had never walked in her direction since, and was reluctant to do so now. Her marriage to the widower Duke of Middlesborough caused very little excitement. This was not surprising. She was forgotten, and as Dukes go her new husband was neither rich nor illustriously born. He had a country house, not an enormous one, and recently acquired, in Hertfordshire, and a town house in Gloucester Place. The title was created by George II. Before him they had been Viscounts since the time of Charles II, and before then wool merchants. Charles ennobled them for contemptible reasons, so it says in history books, and George II duked them in exchange for cash down, or something very like it. Their money was misdirected during the Industrial Revolution, and though the family, who were called Gilledon, still owned a good deal of it, they were no longer millionaires as they had once been. Harriet's husband had about £6000 a year. He was not young, about fifty, and he was not interesting. The marriage was quietly celebrated in a Registry Office. Georgie had not much to tell me about it when I asked her.

"I think Harriet tried very hard," she said, "but she couldn't fit into the life of India."

"But she and her husband seemed so devoted," I said.

"Oh, they were at first. But he's an archaeologist, and can you see Harriet as a companion for an archaeologist?

And don't forget to look at it from his point of view either. My dear, he must have found her exasperating! No wonder he got bored and went off with someone else."

"Did he?"

"He had a mistress. An Indian woman. Poor Harriet was frightfully shocked. She divorced him."

Georgie did not pursue the subject, and this was so unlike her that I guessed that the whole affair must have been extremely painful. I learned about it a few weeks later.

I saw a man coming out of the Oxford and Cambridge Club in Pall Mall. He was conscientiously rather than smartly dressed, and I knew him, but not who he was. He looked healthier than the ordinary Londoner, and I guessed from his piercing look at me that he, like I, was trying to remember where in the world we had met. It was Vereker. As we shook hands, we made the usual remarks. I asked him if he was free for dinner one night.

"Yes, any night this week after Wednesday," he said.

"Then let's have dinner one day this week in my flat."

His eyes lit up. "I'd like that," he said, "particularly if you have a piano as, needless to say, you must have. I'd like to hear you play again."

"Not on your life," I said. "This time we'll hear real music for a change. By wonderful luck I have a couple of tickets for Toscanini at the Queen's Hall. He's doing the Seventh Symphony. It ought to be superb!"

"Oh, I'd like to hear a concert. The Seventh Symphony. Beethoven?"

"Yes. Come on Friday, about half-past six if you can.

We'll have sandwiches, then Toscanini, then supper at home."

When the evening came round I was amused to notice how it resembled our piano festival in Jaideri; how the incidents grouped themselves round Toscanini's rendering of the Seventh, as they had once done round my inept caricature of some of that work. In music, which he loved with such a beautiful passion, Vereker was a small child.

He wanted to know all about the Seventh, and I told him the things which are written in programmes: how in form this is considered the most perfect of Beethoven's symphonies, but that many people regard the Third and Ninth as greater achievements; how Wagner had described it as "the apotheosis of the dance"; and so on; and these ancient remarks deeply interested him. We reached the Queen's Hall in good time. The first part of the programme was taken up by the Coriolan Overture, and the Sixth, the second with the immortal Seventh. As at Jaideri the first bout of listening moved him so much that he was hardly able to speak, either between the items or in the interval, while the second bout appeared to make him feel strangely at peace with the world, so that when we were back in my flat again he was in a communicative mood. At supper he told me a lot about affairs in Siwandistan and the North West Province, told it well in his dry precise way, every now and again, stopping, laying a hand on my arm, with such words as: "That bit in the middle of the slow part of the Seventh — how does it go?" And I would hum it. I may make him seem rather absurdly simple, but if so I am wrong.

He was a very intelligent interesting man who, since boyhood, had been cut off from every form of cultured life.

Then as we sat by the fire after supper, with a whisky and soda each, I asked him about the Homers: "What on earth was all that about? It must have begun soon after I left."

There was something prim about Vereker, I knew, but I was surprised at the degree of primness which he now showed. He pursed his lips. "Yes, soon after," he said, and then added: "Shocking, shocking, shocking."

"I've known her a long time, and I like her in a way. But I can imagine it happening, poor thing."

"You can imagine — " he cried, and then in a quiet voice. "Oh, well, I never knew her well, so it came to me as a very great surprise indeed." He seemed to be rather shaken by my remark.

"Who was Homer's mistress?" I asked.

"Homer's mistress?"

"Yes. She divorced him because he had a mistress, so her sister told me. Isn't that right?"

"No, it is not," he said shortly.

"Well, what did happen?"

Since the conversation had drifted to the East, Vereker had shown more of the reserved manner I knew; he was once more acting his fine part. He lit a cigarette and paused before answering, and when he did so he spoke in his measured way.

"Look here, when I spoke just now, I assumed you knew all about it. It was a very unpleasant business, but I see no need to spread scandal. I'd rather not go into it."

I now really wanted to know.

"I often see her sister and her friends. I'm sure to hear in the end. I might as well know everything now."

Vereker indicated by a subtle smile that he was not taken in by this protestation, and saw through it into my pleasure in gossip. But, I suppose because our experiences together at the Queen's Hall had made us intimate friends once more, he told me. The facts, though odd, were simple enough. But I fancy that to Vereker, who knew nothing of Harriet's early life, they were often more puzzling than they were to me. I could fill some gaps in the tale with informed guesswork.

Unlike most simple people Harriet had small capacity to love. She knew little about her own nature, nothing about life; when she was very young she was bewildered, wearied, and even sickened by the ceaseless desire with which she was surrounded. Like most simple people she thought that she could be rescued by the complement of a robust intelligence. Most of the people she met were stupid, and she wanted to escape from them, but did not know how to do so, and she was timid. At last she found her chance, and in so far as she could, with her dull nature, she fell in love with Homer. She thought he had what she needed and loved him for that. She was wrong. He fell in love with her but never awakened her. I do not believe that she could be awakened; she suffered from a sort of sleeping sickness of the soul. Archaeology is not an exciting occupation if the past means nothing to you at all, indeed under those circumstances it is far less exciting than coal-mining, and so it followed inevitably that Harriet was bored by Homer's interests. India is a wonderful place, but it is hot, uncomfortable, and the poverty of the crowd is repellent. It is no place for person defective in imagination, sympathy, or patience, and Harriet was defective in all three: her patience was of a self-centred unintelligent kind. So she soon became bored by India. Homer gave her a deep romantic love, and she returned this love as long and as well as she could. If they had had children they might have settled down to a kind of happiness, but something went wrong there; she had a series of miscarriages, and after a short time they were forced to accept the fact of childless marriage. Harriet lacked the natural generosity necessary to adapt herself to an unnatural or frustrated life. When the transports of physical passion subsided her love for Homer vanished, and then turned into a feeling of shocked disappointment. She saw that she had made a mistake, and that she should have followed the original plan, as her sister had done. She began to brood on means of escape, like a prisoner.

She had met the Duke of Middlesborough in her débutante days before he was a widower, and he had cast many lecherous glances at her. About six months before my visit to Jaideri the duke had stayed there for a week in the course of a sporting tour. He saw a great deal of Harriet. He made love to her in the course of doing which he fell in love with her; he grew desperate and asked her to run away with him. Though she was far too conventionally respectable to run away she did not resist his advances with absolute refusal. In her brooding she had already faced the unpleasant fact that she could only escape by divorce, and all the scandal which that step involved; but she wanted to be the innocent party. She was bourgeois, as she had always been. She did not love the duke, as she had once loved Homer, but, as with Homer, she saw in him a symbol of salvation. She did not encourage him, but she submitted to a few embraces. Before he left, when he made a last appeal to her to go with him, she told him that one day she might be free, and that if that happened she might marry him. He said he would wait for her. He did.

Homer remained so fixed in love that she could not even discuss the possibility of a divorce with him. He loved her more than he had done when they were first married. I can imagine that that happened through a sort of triumph of her dumbness. Her dumbness was so absolute that if you refused to describe it as stupidity you might see in it depth and mystery. His love oppressed her, made her prison more close and terrible. She suffered much from it, and suffering at last made her cunning. The stupidest prisoners devise clever ways of escape.

Bishop was the blot on the English Society of Jaideri. It was true, as he let me find out, that he was an able man with a fatally weak character, and with no sensitiveness to moral values or conventions. He was a petty swindler despised by every one who knew him, English and Indian; his standards of honesty were lower than those of the bazaars. He had not even the common virtue of rogues, defiant courage. This much I knew, but there was a little more. He was under a heavy obligation to Vereker who had saved him from a long term of imprisonment. He had been discovered not only to be keeping a brothel, but to be attempting blackmail on young officers whom he had lured to this paradise. Vereker had discovered the scandal in time to close it without proceeding to the further scandal of a case damaging to English prestige. The affair was hushed up, but every one knew of it. No one ever talked about it, not even men in clubs. At the time, the governing authorities wanted to send Bishop elsewhere, but Vereker intervened, because he, like myself, was moved to pity by this broken man. He was determined to give Bishop a second chance. The authorities gave in to him. He was much criticized for his action, at first, but the fact that Bishop became involved in no further major scandal seemed, in the end, to vindicate his protector. None the less it was, in every one's opinion, a humiliation for the Homers to be rescued by this contemptible man. Unfortunately there was no one else equally capable of helping them.

It will be remembered that when I was waiting for Harriet and Bishop at Shabbareg they arrived a day late. This was because they stopped on the way. There was a house belonging to a pistachio merchant, about fifteen miles from the road, which was comfortable by Pathan standards. Here Harriet and Bishop stopped, and Bishop became her lover. When the Homers were together again in Jaideri Harriet told her husband what had happened. She said she was in love with Bishop. For some time he thought she was joking. At last he realized that she was speaking seriously. There is no need to describe the horrible scenes which followed in the next few days as his love for his wife turned into helpless hatred and despair. She said he could divorce her citing Bishop as her lover. In the end she divorced him. He found an Indian prostitute who posed as his mistress. He was left in India alone. The fury of the English in Jaideri against Bishop was more violent than it had ever been before, even than on the occasion of the brothel scandal, and Vereker could now do nothing for him, though he wanted to. He saw through Harriet. Bishop was obliged to seek his living in some other province. This meant irrecoverable financial loss to him. Harriet went home to England, and as soon as permissible married the Duke of Middlesborough.

Those were the facts. The oddest one of all, to my mind, was the incredible degree of skill shown by Harriet as she played out her heartless scheme. Her choice of Bishop as her instrument showed a knowledge of human nature which would have been remarkable in a person of brilliant cleverness. He was perfectly suited to her purpose. She knew that he was pusillanimous, and would do as he was told if told firmly. She knew that no normal man could resist an invitation to go to bed with her, but she knew too that this one would never dare claim her as his woman, or make a jealous scene. But her craft showed at its keenest in the fact that she so accurately estimated her husband's mind. When confronted by the treacherous destruction of his home from within he could not bear to commit the act of vengeance which was his due. He could not bear the public shame of Bishop as his wife's lover, and so, rather than that, he allowed himself to appear as the guilty party. She owed everything to her flawless choice of lover. I remembered Bishop's pitiful attempt to look smart and dashing when he called on me the evening of our return to Jaideri. I believe, looking back on our talk then, that he had just called on her in his new character of lover, and been told where he got off. And he had got off, wretched man.

Harriet had probably not guessed that in their rage at Bishop, the English colony of Jaideri would forget to blame her, for this was difficult to foretell. She took a risk here, and won a large bonus. Vereker alone kept his head, and I gathered from one or two of his remarks that he had suffered much unpopularity for blaming her in part, and for "sticking up as usual for that filthy little pet of his."

I have never known whether to marvel at Harriet's hidden criminal cunning, or at her insensitive persistence. On the whole I incline to believe she had more insensitiveness than wickedness in her. She knew that it was wrong to commit adultery. I rather doubt whether she saw anything wrong in the rest of her performance. She could go through with it to the end, not because she was hardened by evil, but because she knew nothing about pain. She could fool herself into supposing that her husband would be happier married to someone more suitable, and that Bishop was too degraded to be worth bothering about, and so she inflicted incurable wounds on both, believing that they would not mind. Her perfect touch was due to the fact that she had no feeling in her finger ends. The smug neatness of what she did was detestable, but in it lay the wonder of her life. She made a mistake when she was young because she thought she could be awakened by the love of an intelligent man, and so she left the pathway so carefully marked out for her. She realized her mistake before she had to contend with age, before there were too many difficulties in the way of a return. When she realized that, she returned the directest way, straight back, destroying two lives. There was magnificence in her total lack of weakness.

The story of Saint George should lead to a picture of the honourable knight, and his goodly esquire, most nobly leaving the maid whom he loved and rescued because she was promised to another, but this performance ended with a small photograph in *The Tatler* of the Duke and Duchess of Middlesborough coming out of a Registry office, because no church could bless such a union. I enjoy, as every one does, complications, and scandals, and disguised evil, and unpredicted virtue, but when I think of my faithful vigil at Shabbareg I often want to exclaim: Oh Life, why can't you sometimes be more like a novelette!

☼ *Me and My Brother*

"FLORENCE," I said, "I want to change my driver. I don't like that man."

"What's wrong with Phillip?"

"Everything. He's no use. Give me another."

"You don't know how to treat him, that's all. He's a very good type. I know my Tamils and you won't find a better one."

I sighed and sat down looking helplessly at Mrs. Raikes. She had a face like a horse, though this did not give her the pathetic expression of docility usual in that cast of feature. She was a bully and had a far stronger character than most people. She was a Houyhnhnm without any of the lofty grace of those fabulous beings. She was about forty-five.

"You need to be rough with boys like Phillip," she said, "you need to trip them up and keep them in their place. Don't allow any sort of familiarity. Make him respect you as a white man."

"Will that make him drive better?"

"Of course it'll make him drive better." She gave me a swift suspicious look. She disliked jokes.

"Florence, I'm afraid I'm a little old to learn how to

treat the Tamils. Can't you get me a perfectly ordinary Indian, or a Persian?"

This was not the first time we had had this argument and I could see that its repetition was making her impatient.

"It's very difficult to find good chauffeurs. I take great pains to get reliable people, and I am the judge as to who is eligible for Legation service. You might get someone who drives better than Phillip, and he might be a spy."

"Phillip is so wonderfully incompetent that I think we may safely say that he cannot be a spy." I gave up.

Mrs. Raikes was the wife of an officer in the Army of India. The conversation recorded above took place in Tehran in the Autumn of 1941. Her husband was on service at Singapore. A few years before the war Major and Mrs. Raikes had spent some months in Shiraz when he was granted language leave from India, and they had both learned to speak Persian fluently. Through the good offices of friends in the Indian Civil Service, which used to supply Consuls to Eastern Persia, she obtained war-work in our Legation in Tehran soon after her husband left India with his regiment. She was made Administration officer. She was very competent; she discharged her functions very well. She ran a fleet of motor cars and a team of drivers between the Legation and the Consulates. Inevitably I met her in the course of my duties soon after I had arrived in Tehran to take up a Legation post.

She and I were not made for each other. I don't think she liked the look of my face, and I did not admire hers. She made it clear that she had no use for my character, and in a short time I found that I entertained similar feelings about hers. I found that I regarded her with a mixture of disapproval and boredom in which boredom was uppermost. I saw her case roughly as follows: the villians who act parts on the stage of the world need to be changed every so often, or else the unending play would become monotonous. During the greater part of recorded time, for example, kings and courtiers made stirring and interesting figures of iniquity, but their hour passed, of necessity, when the abuse of power was no longer the eternal temptation which led them into crime. Their place has been taken by many in turn, but none of the substitutes have stayed. Nowadays we are amused, not moved to terror and pity, by wicked earls, by ruthless financiers, or harsh British Imperialists; they are not modern dangers. A very short time ago, so it seemed to me, people like Mrs. Raikes had been among the threats to civilization; but now she was just an antiquated absurdity. She was the extremest kind of old-fashioned colour-conscious tyrant. Everything said against English rule and the British Empire had been justified by Mrs. Raikes; but now, after it was over, what a bore it was to have to get into a rage about Blimp while there were so many worse things threatening the world!

"We've let things slip in this country," she said to me one day in Tehran. "Giving in, climbing down, truckling. What they want is firm rule."

"I rather doubt it, Florence. They got firm rule from the old Shah. They found it most painful."

She liked to talk about the past.

"I remember when I was a girl no coloured man dared get into the same car, or the same lift in a hotel, as an

Englishman. He would never have dreamed of asking a white girl to dance."

"I am glad to say, and you must be glad to learn, that in Persia these ferocious customs have never arisen. Coloured men are so rare here that colour-consciousness has never got hold of people as it has done elsewhere."

She gave me a contemptuous look. "Perhaps we needed it. Perhaps that's why we've been so sloppy," she said with a defiant air. "Perhaps that's why we've lost Persia." She always talked as though Persia was, or recently had been, a province of the British Empire. In spite of the fact that, knowing the language, she could converse easily with whomever she chose, she remained ignorant because her mind was stuffed to bursting with fixed ideas. She had expected the Persians to be a swarthy primitive race living under the protection of the Union Jack, and she had never been able to adjust her mental faculties to different realities. "The old policy out there wasn't sloppy, I can tell you," she went on. "If a local bigwig had offended the Raj he was compelled to come into the Resident's office on all fours. If a native wouldn't get off the pavement for an Englishman, the Englishman kicked him off; if he kept his umbrella up he tore it in pieces. The native got justice with the lash. That's what the Empire used to be like."

"It sounds delicious. I wish I'd been there."

A poisonous woman, I decided. I began to see why hatred of England can drive some people literally mad. With indignation I tried to imagine what sort of life would have to be lived by a sensitive man of India who found himself in a state of subjection to this brutal and inferior creature. Then I began to change my mind. It was her conduct in the Phillip affair which made me realize that I was seeing her in too simple terms. She wasn't really brutal at all. She was even a rather good-hearted soul. All this talk about kicking people and tearing up umbrellas was in fact nothing more than a perennial daydream of hers in which, perhaps with a violent touch of sexual maladjustment, she indulged her longing to domineer.

Phillip was a Christian native of Madras who had come to Persia as a workman on some temporary job connected with the Anglo-Persian Oil Company. When his job was finished he came to Tehran in search of further employment, and, having heard that Mrs. Raikes had lived in India, he applied to her. She immediately took him into her team of chauffeurs, because he was a Tamil, and, as the reader may recollect, she knew her Tamils.

He was pitch black. I am fortunate (by circumstance rather than character I suppose), in having no aversion to "colour," no instinctive resort to the "colour-bar." In so far as I give way to prejudices in this matter of colour, I do so in that medieval fashion which still survives in Persia: I tend to look upon black people as magical, as weird and strange, and as omens of luck. When Phillip was appointed to drive me whenever I was sent on tour by the Minister, my disposition was to like him. But I soon found myself trying, forcing myself, to like him, until in turn I found this undertaking too much for me. In the end I gave free rein to my dislike. He was so horrible that at moments I even began to wonder whether there was not some sense in Mrs. Raikes's view of the world.

His unpunctuality was most conveniently measured in days. An early start having been delayed to noon, one was sometimes well advised to postpone departure to the next morning, if there was nowhere comfortable to stop on the way. Though he was not a spy, as Mrs. Raikes rightly perceived, he was anxious to make a spy of me. Those were the days of disorder following the Shah's abdication, and it was important for members of Legations to do whatever they could to restore calm. For some time Phillip never failed to tell the nervous populations of Persian towns and hamlets that I was a Secret Intelligence agent engaged in organizing an extension of the horrors of war to these regions. When I told him not to say this, he informed the next population that he had orders not to say what his master was doing, as his master was highly placed in the Secret Service. On another occasion he told the people that the policy of our Legation was to seize Persia and make it a fief of the British throne, whereafter the Persians would all be our abject slaves. This was not said maliciously, but as part of a sincere attempt at pro-British propaganda.

He was not intelligent. He was not honest. He was also without charm. When I taught him the difference between the words "house," "office," "hotel," "caravanserai," "coffee-house," he, as though purposely to exasperate me, used the word "flat" for all these things. "Would you like to stop at this flat?" he would ask as we approached some wind-swept hovel miles away from anywhere. Within doors he was equally skilled in the creation of annoyance. His table manners were such as to make tempting meals uneatable. He ate with the aid of a clasp knife, making the maximum noise and showing as much as possible of the process of mastication.

Finally, he was unable to drive. Throughout our long journeys I was obliged to take the wheel except when the desire to sleep made my driving even more dangerous than his naturally was at all times. This made my very fatiguing official tours almost intolerably exhausting. I did not like Phillip.

Sometimes I used to work out some rather unscrupulous ways of getting rid of him. I fancied that if I went to Mrs. Raikes and put my complaints on a colour-basis, I might get her sympathy. If I had said that, staying in caravanserais and so on, it was impossible to live except on terms of familiarity, and that to do this with a coloured man was bad for the prestige of the Raj, I dare say that Mrs. Raikes would have been moved to action on my behalf. I could not bring myself to do this, however, and I am not sure now whether the ruse would have had the intended effect or not. Phillip, who brought out everything ill-tempered in me, brought out what was fine in her. It was pleasant to see how genuinely kind she was to him. She liked chatting to him in halting Tamil, she liked finding out about his family in Madras, and was prepared to go to much trouble on their account, whenever he wished. I dare say she really did know her Tamils and was deeply interested in them. Because she was stupid she did not let this make her generous-minded, but it did make her behave in a Christian way to Phillip.

"When they respect you, these people give you no trouble," she said.

"I never knew before how thoroughly unrespectable I am."

During October my work included many travels. The Minister was using me partly as a liaison officer between the Legation and some of the Consulates, and partly as an Intelligence Officer. About the middle of October I was ordered to go to Meshed to discuss matters with the new Consul General, and from there to go to Yazd, where we had no Consulate, and then to Isfahan, and so back to Tehran. This meant a very long journey, as Meshed is about six hundred miles from Tehran, and Isfahan nearly eight hundred miles from Meshed. It was before starting on this huge trip that I made my last appeal to Mrs. Raikes. It was useless, as I have indicated.

On the way to Meshed Phillip committed a crime which, it seemed to me, would even shake Mrs. Raikes's confidence in the man. He burgled a house. A merchant put me up for the night and while my host and I were at supper, Phillip went upstairs and removed an acetylene lamp from the merchant's bedroom and stowed it away in the car. I discovered the theft in time to restore the property to the rightful owner. When we reached Meshed I sent a telegram to Mrs. Raikes explaining what had happened. I said that I wished for her authority to dismiss Phillip at Isfahan and obtain a new man from the Consulate there, or from the missionaries. I decided to take him to Isfahan because, bitterly as I disliked him, I did not relish the idea of leaving Phillip adrift in so distant a place as North East Persia.

I spent three days in Meshed. When the Consul General had done with me I left for Yazd.

The whole story depends upon the following circumstance. Persia is a country split in two by an enormous desert called Dasht-i-Lut. This desert extends from the Northern provinces right down to the South. Within it is empty. Now the ancient city of Yazd, in the very middle of Persia, is near to the western fringe of this terrible uninhabited place, and to reach it from Meshed used to be a very long labour, necessitating a journey right round the eastern and southern edges of the Dasht-i-Lut. But in the time of Reza Shah a road was built direct from Meshed to Yazd, straight across the desert at its least broad point. By this road you enter the desert about three hundred miles southwest of Meshed at a place called Tabas, which was the original home of the Tabby cat. After Tabas you see no house till you reach the hamlets lying about Yazd. This road reduces the original journey of over fifteen hundred miles to one of not much more than five hundred. But the journey remains one of the most difficult in Persia; the road is very rough and often needs skilful driving, while you are always conscious of the fact that if you break down you have nowhere to go to for help. It is necessary either to travel in convoy or to be assured that traffic is coming behind you. If it is not one of the heroic journeys of the world, it is certainly not one to be done carelessly.

My first business was to find a guide (because the road is sometimes indistinct) and the Indian garage proprietor who was repairing my car found me one. The guide was called Hassan Baba Ali. He seemed a nice young man. He told me that he was a citizen of Yazd and had just done the pilgrimage to the shrine of Meshed. He said that he had done the journey from Yazd to Meshed several times and knew the road very well. In return for a lift home he would joyfully guide us. We arranged to set out for Tabas early next morning.

The next morning, of course, meant the next afternoon, and I was a little disappointed to find that Hassan Baba Ali was less punctual than Phillip. The latter was ready at a quarter to twelve, only four hours after time, which was remarkable, while Hassan did not appear till half an hour later than this. We stowed away his trunk, a red box on little legs and decorated with metal ornaments, and left Meshed. We went out into that vast grim landscape in which the city stands, and we looked back at the golden dome and the blue dome.

There is no great difficulty in finding the road to Tabas but we took at least three wrong turnings. This was because I gave more weight to the directions of our guide than to the evidence of the map. The third of our wrong turnings was due to a perfectly childish mistake. I sharply inquired of Hassan Baba Ali whether he had in fact ever done this journey before.

"Oh, yes, Aga, indeed I have," he said. "About five times. But I have always gone round the desert, never straight across."

So that was that. The man had never been on the road before.

"But it doesn't matter," said Hassan Baba Ali, "for after all you have a map."

"You hold your tongue."

The danger of living in a sea of falsehood impressed itself anew on my mind. Why was I so sure that a couple of lorries were really coming on behind me next day? Because the Consulate had said so, but did I know that they had been told the truth? They had told me that the Indian garage proprietor was reliable, and he had given me a fraudulent guide. It was absurd to feel frightened about nothing, but I felt very uneasy none the less. I had half a mind to change my plans and go by the long safe southern route. I was not too far advanced on my journey for this to be unpractical. But no! Why should I be done out of a great adventure by two asses? We drove on westwards.

As you come to within fifty miles or so of Tabas you begin to see signs of the desert about you. In Persia you become used to the fact that habited places are usually far from each other, rare spots of green in a tawny landscape, but here we began to see only naked earth. Stretches of immense stony waste, distant sharp hills. Ranges hove in sight far off, then sank away. The sun was setting as we entered the outer regions of this fearful place, and two hours before we were near Tabas it was dark. The road was still easy to follow. The stars shone with uninterrupted brilliance as though through pure space, and they showed so low on the horizon that sometimes we might have thought they were the lights of houses, but that we knew there were none. It was intensely cold. The road grew rougher as it became removed from the scarce comforts of eastern Persia. I thought with some slight relief that no robbers could subsist in this far place. And then, when we had been going in the dark for what seemed a long time, lights appeared in too close a mass to be stars, and after what seemed a long time again, we drove past orchards and walls, and so into the little town of Tabas. We went to the main caravanserai and drove into the courtyard. We were very tired.

Phillip and Hassan shared a room, while I set up my bed on the broad raised platform from which the rooms led off, and went to sleep under the stars. I was awakened by the glow of a light on the other side of the courtyard. It looked like one of those long Chinese-like lanterns which the Persians use, and it was being held very still by someone. As I awoke more I saw that it was the moon and I fell asleep again. The next time I awoke it was on account of the cold, and the moon was high over the world filling the whole sky with light. Orion was near the zenith. I pulled my sheepskin coat over my bed and enjoyed the wonderful scene about me. It was the time of Ramadhan, and a muezzin chanted the prayer before dawn, in the slow and bitterly tragic music of Persia. I fell asleep again. When I awoke the third time there were streaks of light in the east. It was nearly five. I got up and went to call Phillip. Even Phillip was punctual on that morning. Even that dull-witted fool knew that the desert must be crossed by day. We left a little after half-past five.

I noticed that after half an hour or so we took to looking back at the town at intervals. It looked so safe and friendly, and before us stretched the inhuman misery of the desert. It was a long time before Tabas disappeared.

When we stopped for a snack I noticed the silence. Here was what the whole world would look like after doomsday, and what it once looked like, before man, in primeval drought. The noise of Phillip eating a pastry and drinking tea had a kind of terrible improbability about it. There was no other such sound within many miles. Our voices sounded singular in the same way. There were no other voices, not even the voices of animals, hardly the voices of insects. It was strange to think that if one was left there, one would turn into sand. In the eye of eternity it would seem like a drop of water falling into a pool.

One gets used to anything with time, and after an hour or so we were used to the desert, or rather we found ourselves able not to think about it more than was necessary to the purpose. We drove slowly, and because the surface of the Dasht-i-Lut is stony, the road, though very rough, was not difficult to hold. It began to grow hot; the lovely colours of dawn vanished before the single dazzling colour of noon. The place became ugly. The plains through which we drove shone with a deadly whiteness and the distant hills took on the look of corpses; as though they were the huge rotting hulks of primitive reptiles. The heat here in summer must be devasting for even at this mild time of the year it was difficult to bear. The only sign of life we saw was the skeleton of a donkey. We drove without speaking, grateful for the din of the car, for about a hundred miles.

The road began to zigzag. This puzzled me until I discovered that here, right in the middle of the Dasht-i-Lut, the ground was becoming sandy and the road was following the stony courses wherever they could be found. The road had been designed with great skill to avoid the danger of a car sinking into soft beds. It continued like this for about ten miles until it emerged from a narrow valley into a wide plain once more. It was becoming more and more difficult to follow and one could see wheel tracks going off it on independent ways. Then as we came into the wide plain these separate tracks began to converge on to a point, and this point was marked by a sign of humanity. Standing in the plain like two minute fat headless spectres were two iron tanks. As we neared them we skidded several times. We were running into sand. I stopped the car a few yards from the tanks, and got out to inspect the road.

This was the situation. We were nearly out of the sand, so nearly indeed that sixty or seventy yards beyond the tanks the road came on to hard stony ground once more, but these last sixty or seventy yards went across a deep bed of sand. There were some big wheel tracks across it. A big powerful car could get over it without much danger of sticking, but not a touring car such as mine. It was likely that there was a safe way round, but it might be some way off. It must be looked for. I walked out of the bed and began to explore.

Phillip, as I have said, was not intelligent, and was not a good driver. Hassan Baba Ali, as the reader may have guessed, was not the man to correct these deficiencies. As I trudged off to find a road across the sand, these two men were left alone in the car together. Hassan pointed to the tracks and I heard him say "Look, the road goes straight ahead there," and I heard Phillip say

"Yes, I know, it's quite easy, let's get across," and before I could say or do anything to stop him Phillip started up the car and plunged into the sand . . . He got. about fifteen yards and then stopped with the wheels buried above the axles.

We were stuck.

I ran back. I shouted furious things at Phillip and Hassan Baba Ali. Then I stopped, regretting what I had done. We were three tiny live specks in that boundless scene of death. There was no echo for no hills were near. Shouting voices sounded like little squeaks. To be angry was only ridiculous. We were nothing there.

"We must remain till the lorries arrive," I said. "We will try to dig the car out but we are not likely to succeed."

Neither of them seemed very upset. Neither of them realized just how dangerous our state was unless the lorries arrived punctually the next day. It was about two in the afternoon and the heat was violent. They began to dig.

As a formality, knowing precisely what I would find, I went to the tanks. I see them now as vividly as if I had looked at them today. They stood on a rough wooden platform made in the shape of a table. They were about four feet high and circular, about two foot across. They had little taps. I pounded each one in turn with the side of my fist, and from each I was answered by a hollow bong. I turned the taps. Nothing happened. I looked round and saw Hassan Baba Ali drinking from one of our water bottles. I went and took it from him with a brutal gesture. I put all the water bottles under the tanks in the shade. I said that no one was to drink except with my permission. At the same moment I felt thirsty.

From then on we all felt thirsty.

As far as I was concerned, the digging was worth doing just because it was something to do. It was entirely useless. The bed was deeper than I supposed and as we dug the car merely sank more deeply within it. We spread matting under the car, started the engine, and accelerated in reverse. We sank then a little more. This sand was so deep and soft that the only hope we could have was of being hauled out by a big powerful lorry with a high clearance.

I wondered which was worse, the silence or the thirst. Whenever we stopped digging the silence closed on us like a monstrous physical presence. Once an hour we had little nips at the water bottles. Thirst came back after one minute. I wanted to smoke but didn't dare to for fear of increasing my thirst.

There was a range of craggy mountains about seven miles to our left. On the right and behind us the view was not distant as the ground was broken into little sharp hillocks. Before us the plain could be seen stretching away for about fifteen or twenty miles to another range. I tried to see some trait of life somewhere, even a shrub of camel thorn. It was an utterly desolate scene, it was a picture of Nature damned and never to be redeemed. Then quite suddenly, this spectacle became beautiful. As though the lights had been changed by the turning of a switch the glow of late afternoon shone from every hillside. How well one comes to know that divine moment in the East when the sun is no longer the enemy of the earth! It always comes suddenly, like the turning on and out of lights in a play. It is the best moment. It comes about two hours before sunset. Here in the Dasht-i-Lut it filled me with renewed dread, because it meant that daylight was running short. I have a little, inadequate, but nevertheless real idea of what it must be like to go mad from thirst.

Not long after the glow had settled on the hills I thought I saw a change in the landscape in front. Something was there which was not there before. I looked hard. Then I saw what I was looking for. A long way away there was a little white circle with a little black dot in it at the lower edge. It looked like an eye staring down. With a leap of my heart, I understood what this was. The white circle was dust. The little dot was a car. This must be a car coming from Yazd. I called to Phillip and Hassan Baba Ali. The same thing happened to us all. As soon as we saw the car we no longer felt thirsty. I lit a cigarette.

The car took three quarters of an hour to reach us. It was a huge lorry carrying bales of merchandise to Meshed. We were rescued by being dragged out backwards, and then the driver of the lorry, who knew this road well, showed us a way round the bed on to the stony ground beyond. He told us we could go on safely in the dark as there were no more sand beds. I gave him money and cigarettes and we shook his hand. We could hardly bear to leave him. He was called Abdul Kuhbari, and I shall never forget his name.

Though we had seventy miles to go in the desert the rest of that journey seems short in my memory. It was mostly done in the dark, and when we came to the first of the hamlets on the western side we stopped at the coffee-house for some food, and slept for a few hours. Before dawn we started off again, on a road now most pleasingly ordinary. A little after sunrise we saw trees and orchards stretching in a plain, and four slender arms pointing fiercely to Heaven, the four great minarets of Yazd.

I have not said much about Hassan Baba Ali, and one reason is that though he played a great part in this history, there is very little to say about him. Several of the major philosophers have been worried about the problem of existence: about whether, in fact, things are, or are only apparently. When I think of Hassan I begin to see what they mean. We are sometimes told that there are no "things," there are events. Hassan was a curiously ineffective event. His voice was like the echo of another voice. His handsome Persian eyes were vacant, they seemed to see little of what was to be seen. I cannot imagine that he had more strength than a very weak woman. He seemed to have just enough to keep him wiltingly erect. When he ran he trotted in a ladylike way with his hands folded over the lower part of his stomach. I do not believe he consciously deceived me when he offered himself as a guide, for I do not believe that he was conscious of anything in a high degree. Yet, though to all appearances he was so weak and futile, he was lovable. The effect on him of this journey proved that. When he found himself back so soon in his home in Yazd he was filled with gratitude to Phillip and me, with gratitude so strong and beautiful that it enabled him to transform our relationship. He said he would like to call on me at my caravanserai and I appointed him five o'clock that day.

The English often fail to maintain chance friendships because they are not so lavish in their customs as other people. The streak of modesty in our character, which lies in such strange juxtaposition to our unquenchable vanity, is too often carried into our notions of hospitality. I knew that when Hassan Baba Ali came at five o'clock he would come with some of his family, and for the sake of what we had endured I did not want to disappoint him, so I ordered tea and cakes enough for half a dozen, and a bottle of arak in case they were not strict about wine. I failed, of course, as we always fail. At least fifteen arrived and I did what I could to get more food and tea while they pretended not to notice.

While travelling I had worn my military uniform as I thought this might help in dealing with robbers. This had inspired Phillip to spread a rumour in Yazd that I was a British general with a large army at my beck and call, and that I was travelling in order to make preliminary arrangements for conquest. Belief in this story seized hold on the town, and so the family of Hassan Baba Ali treated me with extravagant respect. I saw what was in their minds from the way they addressed me, but my efforts to disabuse them were mistaken for subtlety and cunning. We had a long tea party. Between bouts of conversation we sat smiling at each other in the silent fashion of Persia. We talked about the war and I told them what I could of the news. I was looked upon with affection as it was assumed that a feature of my forth-coming conquest would be the protection of Yazd from the Russians.

"And where is the other gentleman honourably be-stowing himself?" asked Hassan Baba Ali.

"You mean Phillip?"

"Yes, Aga."

"He's cleaning the car."

At the end of my tea party Hassan told me that his father wished to meet me, and had dared ask whether I would deign to honour him at supper the next night. I said I would much like to meet him. Then they rose to go, and I accompanied them to the gate of the court-yard, they bowing and protesting that I should not exert myself so excessively. They asked before leaving what time I wanted supper and we agreed for half-past eight. They would come to fetch me, they said. I shook hands all round, and we parted.

I had a long and wonderful sleep. I spent the next day concluding my official business, returning to the caravan-serai in time for a shave before the supper party, and at half-past eight the deputation arrived bearing lanterns. Hassan Baba Ali led them, and Phillip was among them. I gave them tea and we set forth.

Yazd is one of the lovely cities of the world, and this is partly because it has a particular form of house which is charming and comfortable. There is a courtyard gar-den with a row of rooms on two, and sometimes three but never on four sides. In the wall of the court opposite to the main room there is a large recessed arch, built in much the same style as the recesses in mosque. This is the main meeting place in the summer months. Yazd is a town beautifully designed to make life pleasant in hot weather. All the houses have "wind towers," broad high structures like chimneys made to catch the wind and convey a draft within, and when the tower is open you hear the wind echoing within it. To such a house we now went in procession. We were taken to the main room, as it was considered too cold to eat in the recessed place without.

Seated on a chair was the father of Hassan Baba Ali, a grave noble figure with a white beard and a skull cap on his head. On his right and on his left were empty chairs, little ones with velvet seats from which hung bobbles. There was a row of seats along one wall, and the only other furniture was a table covered with a lace cloth on which stood sweetmeats and fruit. Behind the father of Hassan there was what I can best describe as a bank of human beings. This was the family. I find it difficult to guess numbers. I suppose there could not have been as many as forty, but there must have been at least thirty unless my memory has grown distorted. The point is there seemed to be hundreds. They were men, boys, and little children of both sexes, but no grown women. The children were the most numerous and they all sat on the floor. Most of the boys and men sat on the floor too, though several were seated on chairs, and several stood, giving this great crowd something of the appearance of a bank of flowers. From without came noises of the kitchen at work.

I said Salaam from the door and there was a subdued murmur as the greeting was returned. I then went forward as the old man rose, and I extended my hands to him. He ceremoniously greeted first me and then Phillip, using both hands as is the custom on serious occasions. He then invited me to sit on the chair on his right, and Phillip on the other. There was a pause, broken by little whisperings. Hassan Baba Ali and the others crept in and sat on chairs by the wall. After this pause, which seems to be a kind of courtesy, the old man turned to me.

"It is a great honour to receive your lordship in this house," he said.

"It is an honour for me to sup with the father of my friend," I replied.

He then inquired about my health, and I about his. He asked after the King of England, wanting to know whether he was satisfied with the war, and what religion he followed. He added further protestations that it was an honour to receive me thus, and I answered with deference. He then turned to his other guest and told him that the house and its contents might be considered now as the property of Phillip and me, a proposition to which Phillip assented. He said, "Yes, all right," in Persian. Hassan Baba Ali presented us with sweetmeats and fruit, and a man came in with cups of tea for the guests and the principal members of the family. The majority remained unoccupied, seated or standing, gazing at us in silent wonder. We now entered a definite and recurrent cycle of entertainment: sweetmeats, tea, conversation. When our preliminary politenesses were over, talk become more lively. We discussed the affairs of the country, argued gently, and made jokes. Every now and again the veiled figures of women would peep in from the darkness of the courtyard, and vanish in a flurry if I caught their eyes. Phillip was awed by the scene and only spoke when spoken to. This was a very good thing indeed.

It is the custom in Persia for the guest to propose meat, not the host as with us, so after an hour of tea and conversation I asked the father of the house if he was ready for supper. He asked, anxiously, if I was hungry. I said Yes, I was ready to eat. He issued an order to Hassan Baba Ali.

"Get the table ready."

I was uncertain as to what was going to happen. Though the din of the kitchen was ever audible I saw none of the usual signs of a forthcoming repast, and the table with the lace cover, on which the sweetmeats had stood, was not large enough to accommodate many. Yet the father of the house had said that the table was to be prepared for supper. I had noticed that this household was run in the old Persian style, far more so than is usual in that country among people of means. The intrusion of a European had somewhat thrown them out, that was clear. In the old style supper is eaten on the floor with the hands, but now the table was being laid with cutlery, and when this was finished a tureen of soup and two bowls were placed upon it, and Hassan Baba Ali announced in a respectful whisper that supper was ready. The father of the house made motions for me to go to the table. I was at sea.

"Your supper is ready," he said.

I rose up. I expected him to follow but he remained seated and made motions to Phillip to follow my example, which he did.

"Are you not eating too, Sir?" I said to the father.

"Later. Supper is now ready for your lordship and your brother."

Phillip was my brother.

The room was a large one, about twenty-five feet by fifteen. In the centre of it Phillip and I sat down to supper, while at the far end there remained our large, silent, and appreciative audience.

In former ages, to be accorded the right to eat in public was accounted among the highest marks of distinction; it was a kingly privilege, and, even so late as the time of Louis the Sixteenth, the King of France could be viewed at table from a gallery; nor do I know of any evidence that he regarded this as a tiresome intrusion on his privacy. On the contrary, he seems to have taken pleasure in the custom. I belong to a different generation. Petty as it may be, I prefer to eat in closed chambers, and I found this act of public nourishment embarrassing, indeed I found it so disturbing that it took away my hunger. The usual Persian custom is to eat in silence, and this increased the ordeal, for the noises of eating stood out prominently in the room, and, as I have already said, Phillip was not delicate at the board. As I gazed at black Phillip hissing and sucking over his soup, I remembered the name of Mrs. Raikes. That thought brought other ones in its wake.

To this day I can only guess why these kind and excellent people thought that Phillip was my brother. Presumably they imagined that my father had two wives: an English one, my mother, and a dark one, Phillip's. It is unlikely that Phillip told them that this was the case, because the black man's rumours, for all their fantasy, were not deliberate lies as a rule; they represented what he sincerely believed; he did not lie for the sake of lying, for he had not sufficient imagination to enjoy that perverted pleasure. It was Hassan Baba Ali, I believe, who had represented us in these terms, because he came of a race of poets. He adorned our life together with this beautiful interpretation, seeing us through grateful eyes as twin saviours. I was moved, though I soon saw how grave were the consequences for me.

One of the great differences between our own civilization and that of the East lies in the different prominence given to the relationship of brothers. There is an Oriental passion for the idea of brotherliness whose origins are not known. The idea may be Islamic, or it may come from some more ancient order. It is widespread and exerts extraordinary influence. Friends adopt each other as brothers, swear oaths of brotherhood, revere the word as much as the word "mother." To call someone "My brother" is like calling him "My darling! My beloved one!" This passionate cult sometimes makes Europeans suppose that Eastern people are more homosexual than Europeans, but I believe this is not so. Of course the cult can easily become confused with homosexual emotions, but as a rule I believe it to be an extension, an extravagant Oriental extension, of family feeling: it explains why, when an Oriental is a good friend, he is the best friend in the world. To find such high poetry as this repulsive, when met in experience, is the mark of an evil disposition. I knew that, and yet I could only regret, more and more, that such honours had come to me at this moment, in this way. For the brotherhood thrust upon me was the end of my comfort: I could never be free of Phillip now. I was indissolubly bound to Phillip. I myself could not raise a finger in my rescue.

Soup was followed by a heap of rice in which were pieces of chicken. Phillip was holding up a leg and hacking at it with his clasp knife. He looked like an ogre feasting on babies.

"Put down your knife, Phillip, and that piece of chicken." I leaned across the table and cut it up for him. "Use your spoon and for God's sake don't make so much noise eating."

He was unable to obey my last injunction, and it probably seemed so queer and unserious to him that he did not try. All the other noises in the room, the echoing laugh of the wind in the tower, and the clatter of pots and pans from without, were inaudible beside the noise of Phillip's eating. The latter sounded rather like the noise of horses struggling through boggy ground. No beast that I have heard made more noise in eating than this human. When his breathing became affected by overloading he uttered little squeaks as he ground away with his teeth. We held the attention of our audience, as we, the wonderful brothers, ate with those many eyes fastened upon us. The family were all infinitely too polite to betray any feelings but those of admiration and interest.

The chicken was followed by roast mutton, eggs, and more rice. Eggs were an unfortunate choice from the point of view of the Phillip question, so much so that when he got busy on them even this self-controlled public gave signs of unsteadiness. I heard the word "Ajeeb" whispered several times. It means "Strange."

"Don't spit, Phillip," I said. "Swallow," for he made short work of what morsels he did not like. I cut up his meat once more. I gave him a gentle kick under the table, caught his eye, and hypnotized him to imitate my use of the spoon, and somehow we got through to the end of the kabob which followed. The restraint of the audience was at length broken when I said that we had had enough; a wail of distress at our meagre appetites went up, but I was firm.

"We have had a fine feast, me and my brother."

When we parted an hour later, at the gate of my cara-vanserai, Hassan Baba kissed Phillip and me, and I kissed him and Phillip.

At the Consulate in Isfahan there was a telegram for me:

IN VIEW PHILLIPS MISCONDUCT AUTHORIZE DIS-MISSAL BUT INSIST YOU ENGAGE TEMPORARY REPEAT TEMPORARY REPLACEMENT FOR JOURNEY TO TEHRAN AS RETAIN FULLEST RIGHT PERMANENT REPEAT PER-MANENT APPOINTMENTS LEGATION STAFF REGARDS RAIKES

With a heavy heart I wrote my reply and gave it for transmission to the Consular clerk.

THANKS AUTHORIZATION WHICH NOW NOT NECES-SARY STOP RETURNING WITH PHILLIP EXPLAIN LATER REGARDS SYKES

The complication of the thing came upon me. Explain later! How? In what terms? With what argument could any one, could even a genius of negotiation, make that monster understand this predicament? If the reader feels with me about this question of brotherhood, which now dominated the situation, then the reader is not Mrs. Raikes. For her there were certain chasms which were not only not bridged, but never should be bridged, for such was the extent of her superstition. That woman with the colour-crazed brain might not have listened to some cock-and-bull story about familiarity in taverns, such as I had vilely toyed with earlier, but she would have very decided views about me and my brother. It was horribly ironical that if I told her the truth, I would be compelled to have what I wanted, to have what, with equal vehemence, I now at the last moment did not want to have at any price. I could hear her voice: "The Tamil is a thoroughly reliable fellow, if you know how to treat 'im. He'll respect Justice, he'll despise sloppiness. Of course I know that in the rough and tumble of the road a lot of give and take is inevitable. It happens in India too, you'll be surprised to hear. But when it comes to members of the King-Emperor's Legation entering into brotherhood pacts, with coloured people, and kissing — ugh — in public, why then I'd say to 'em: here's your ticket home. They may be some use in Whitehall, but they're dash all use out here. And if you really simply can't dispense with their services — ha ha ha — then good-bye the coloured brother, if you don't mind." I tossed and turned on my bed, and had many nightmares of this kind.

A few days later my great journey came to an end in Tehran. I retired for a day to write my report for the Minister, but Mrs. Raikes sought me in my house.

"This business about Phillip. What's it all about? Do you want to keep him on or don't you?"

"I'd rather he was kept on."

"But you say he burgled a house, a house in which you were staying. Disgraceful! Absolutely unforgivable!"

"Yes, awful. But — but — but — Give him another chance."

"He's had his chance. He's let us down. He's a rotter. He ought to be sacked."

"I see your point entirely, but please don't sack him. Not now, at least. I'd much rather you didn't. I — I've taken a fancy to him."

Then she looked at me with new eyes.

"Ah, I know what you mean. The Tamil gets under your skin."

"No, he doesn't. Not Phillip, I mean. I just don't want him to be sacked. It's difficult to explain."

"I know," she said in a low voice, smiling and nodding her head; and speaking in an ever softer, more distant, more beautifully omniscient tone, she went on: "*I* know. *I* know. *I* know."

"No, you don't," I wanted to say, for this was the truth, but instead I weakly repeated, "It's difficult to explain," and over her face there spread a smile which was sincere and full of deep understanding for what she took to be my problem.

☼ *Conflicting Passions*

ONE day in Madrid, during the civil war, a clergyman of the Church of England was seen climbing out of a hotel window on to a fire escape, down which he then began to run as rapidly as he could. A second later, loud explosions echoed in the courtyard. A man was seen hanging out of the window (the same window as that from which the clergyman had emerged), firing a pistol at the descending figure. The assailant was drunk, otherwise his victim must have been killed.

Of course this incident was followed by a great deal of commotion, and the wildest rumours began to fly round as explanations. The final, the "definitive" version of the story was that a political crime had been attempted; it was said that the clergyman, whose sympathies with the Spanish Government were undoubted, had been tracked to his hotel by a Fifth Columnist who was happily too drunk to commit the murder which he intended. I read this story in the papers in England, and was much interested in it, because the clergyman in question, Canon Symonston, was a man whom I knew. He was a respected figure in our cathedral town in the north of England, having held Canonical office there for some years. A few months after reading of his adventure, I met him at a wedding reception and I congratulated him on his escape. He smiled his habitual vacant smile and murmured something about the whole thing being due to some sort of misunderstanding. These seemed to me rather odd words to use. I remember thinking at the time that he probably wished to dismiss so horrible an incident from his memory, and tended to express himself carelessly about it as a result. It was not till long after that I understood what he meant. I learned what really happened, and I relate it now, because I see an important moral in this weird freak of chance. It seems to illustrate a peculiar danger of enthusiasm, (that vice which is now acclaimed as a virtue) to which people may be exposed when they bring burning sympathy alone to the ordinary men and women involved in great upheavals. Inflamed partisans, when they are not directly involved, sometimes forget that no matter for what intoxicating causes men may suffer, crude ordinary life will go on.

In middle age Canon Symonston was caught up in a movement, or rather in a mass of movements, which can be best described as "The Political Left."

To understand how that came about one must remember again the fashionable mental atmosphere of the nineteen thirties, the golden age of theoretical politicians of the advanced schools. Most people who wished to lead vigorous intellectual lives became interested in politics at that time — in fact not to do so was disapproved, and contemptuously described as "escapism" — and the

fashionable direction of this interest was towards the programme of the "Left." To say that you were not of the
Left, in intellectual society then, was almost bold. It
wasn't done.

You did much more surprising things instead. I must
quickly indicate them to show what was the force which
drove the Canon on into the jaws of death.

Having become a Leftist you might become a Marxist,
but usually became a Hegelian: you became a believer
in Group-life, in the Community. Of course you denied
being a Hegelian since you believed you were not a Na-
tionalist, although you affirmed that you wanted to give
national governments powers on a vast scale. The way
out of this confusion was to be found in the fact that
though you revered groups, and saw mankind not as men
but as a set of many-headed monsters, you were very
fussy indeed about what sort of groups, or monsters, you
revered. You scrutinized group-leaders. You said that all
was well provided that leadership was never entrusted to
soldiers, priests, business magnates, or kings, as these were
capitalist and reactionary, and reaction was the mark of
the beast. This last supposition gave rise to some philo-
sophical problems. It had long been known to science
that a man incapable of reactions, into whom you could
stick pins without causing pain, was in a very bad way.
From this was it not logical to suppose that a political
system incapable of reaction was not robustly healthy?
This objection was answered as follows: reaction, in the
political sense, only referred to reactions against the natural changes of progress. If you then objected that the
Fascist systems were terribly natural changes in a prog-

ress from a humane civilization to barbarism, you were told that progress, in the sense of the Left, referred to an ascending scale of justice. Because such a vision agreed with certain theories of evolution, a sequence of increasing justice was supposed to be inevitable. The Italian and German groups had gone wrong because Hitler and Mussolini were anxious to further the interests of soldiers, priests, kings, and business magnates. But a group under Left leadership was not prone to wrong-doing. If you asked what "Left" meant you were told it meant belief in the foregoing or something akin to it. All this was very different from the teachings of Christianity, but it was thought to be more in accord with scientific discovery, and to have superseded our traditional religion.

Such style of thinking looked different then from what it does now. The Left enjoyed power in fewer parts of the world then, and their followers had the heady pleasure of living on air, promise-crammed. Russia, the Holy See of Leftism, was as remote from day-to-day life as Tibet, and the real or supposed opposition of the Left everywhere to their Fascist opponents furnished the programme with the note of heroism. Many people of every description became converted. There was always work for the man at the front, over which one day, quite unexpectedly, there was thrust the head of the Canon asking for the sign of faith.

Because it was a very sudden development, I fancy that for him conversion was an affair of the Damascus Road. A great light seemed to shine. He took a glad exhilarating flight into faith. This development was all the more remarkable because hitherto he had been a very ordinary divine; in fact when I first saw him, in the late nineteen twenties, I remember being surprised at what I can only paradoxically call his very extreme ordinariness, and by this I do not mean he was mediocre, but that he rigorously conformed to type. A chubby face, a dome of near baldness with the transparent aftermath neatly parted in the centre, a rich voice which suggested some pleasing pealing organ playing nothing in particular in a Gothic fane, plump dimpled hands; in short, a stage clergyman if ever there was one.

He had a kind heart, I know. That heart was perhaps wonderfully warmed by learning the simple fact that Karl Marx had preached the cause of the poor, so warmed that his whole nature became filled with a fervour, uncompromising as it was blind, for the new gospel of hate.

In due time he made his pilgrimage to Russia. Because he was modest, and avoided publicity, he was never famous, but after his visit to Russia he had some public life. This consisted in the main of weighty and confusing letters to the Leftist Press demanding fair play for the Soviet, and occasional speeches to local progressives. When the Spanish war came he was a strong partisan of the Spanish Government.

In his view that appalling struggle was entirely simple in character; it was a straight case of black and white, and the participation of Russia, which, unlike other apologists, he never sought to deny but rather strove strenuously to affirm, only made his own side whiter than ever. Throughout the conflict I believe him to have been as ignorant about it as it is possible to be of a mighty event played out before the eyes of the whole world.

Some of his utterances at the time were reported in our Northern paper, and one of them found its way to the Spanish Press. This obscure journalistic event was the prelude. A consequence of his name appearing on the back-page of a Spanish newspaper was that one day he received a large cheap envelope bearing a Spanish stamp, within which was a printed sheet, and a letter in manuscript. He wondered very much what this might be. He remembered that Professor Ratesby, who was fluent in the language, was coming to see him in three or four days' time in the course of a Northern lecturing tour. He would ask him to translate these papers. It would mean delaying the answer but he considered that that did not matter. (It will be seen later that this mattered a great deal.) The professor's visit appeared to him to be a stroke of luck, but in fact it was a misfortune heavily disguised. This encounter led yet further to the attempted assassination.

Professor Ratesby was a prominent figure in fashionable Leftist circles. I remember meeting him from time to time in those days, and in spite of his geniality I never liked him in the way I could not help liking the Canon. You could not doubt the latter's honesty, but something about the professor made me think he was insincere. He had a trick of dragging famous names into his conversation, as though to impress you with the great people he knew, and yet in spite of this apparent familiarity with the inner councils of statesmanship, he never seemed to have anything of interest to say. He was regarded as a great expert on Spanish affairs, but if you asked him to explain what was happening in Spain, he gave you thin propaganda in reply.

He called, as expected, and in the course of the afternoon the Canon gave him the contents of the envelope. He sat over them in silence. Then when he had read the letter, and the paper with it, he walked to the fireplace and drew himself up (he was a tall slender man with prominent teeth), and said "Oh-o." He bent his large intelligent eyes on his companion. "This," he said, "may be not uninteresting. Not," he repeated, "uninteresting."

The Canon waited for him to go on.

"This," said the professor, "is an invitation to you to visit Madrid."

"Indeed! And pray who is it from?"

"I was coming to that." He resumed his glasses which he had slipped into his pocket. "The printed sheet," he said, "which I hold here in my hand, is a manifesto published by 'The Society for the Promotion of Progressive International Contact,' at least," he rather needlessly added, "that is how I translate it into English from the original Spanish!" He paused, breathed, and went on: "And the letter, which I hold here in my other hand, is from the secretary of this organization, who invites you to go out and lecture in Madrid, and also to visit, this is significant, Symonston, also to visit the front line, under their auspices. Not uninteresting."

"Very much not!" exclaimed the Canon. "Indeed this is, to say the least, a moving tribute to my poor efforts. I shall make arrangements to go immediately."

132

"Ah, but that is what we must discuss. Spain is not easily visited, believe me. You have, perhaps, small idea of the difficulties in the way, and of the great quantity of formalities which have to be completed, and of how conscientiously the authorities insist upon them. Do you know Negrin?"

"No. No, I don't."

The professor paused self-consciously before saying in a deep voice: "I *do*." Then he resumed: "It so happens that I myself am accompanying a small delegation to Spain, and we start from London in a fortnight. We are *not* going to Madrid. We are going to Barcelona. But I believe we may help you considerably. I am proposing that you come with us, and then, if you do so, I will see that you are set on your way, once we are in Spain. We are an influential party — not enormously so, but — in-fluential. I strongly recommend that you come with us, and save yourself a very great deal of trouble. If you agree, and if you come to London as soon as possible — I repeat — as soon as possible, to obtain your visa as a member of our party, I shall be able to assist you from the word 'Go.' If necessary I shall arrange for a telegram to be sent to Negrin."

"Do you happen to know the Society for the Promotion of Progressive International Contact?"

"I was coming to that." As though proclaiming something incredibly exciting he said: "I do *not* know them." He then went on: "I fancy they are a not unrecent institution. It is not impossible that I am mistaken, but at all events they were not prominent when I was last in Spain, hardly six months ago. Their address, which I will leave

133

with you, is at a bank, a reputable, well-known bank. That is significant. It may suggest that they are Centre-Left, liberalistic. . . . But what I find reassuring is that it certainly suggests that they are officially approved. That is the main point. I recommend that we get in touch with them in Spain. It is certainly a most interesting overture. If I can arrange for you to be of our party, may I count on you coming with us?"

"Oh, indeed, you may," cried the Canon, "have no doubt about that. I will cancel all other appointments."

"Then I will expect you in London in a few days. I urge you to write immediately for your visa, while I discuss the matter with the Spanish Consulate, which I will do," he added with a mirthful "human" touch, "to-morrow as ever is."

They parted that evening to meet again in London.

Restrictions, which are almost an essential part of our lives now, were rare in those days, and for many people the Spanish war provided the scene where the great modern chains were first seen and heard. Entry into the country, and movement within it, were severely supervised. It seemed lucky for the Canon that he travelled as a privileged person in a delegation of politicians. It seemed lucky too that among their number should be the powerful Professor Ratesby. Had he been less bountifully assisted the Canon would not have found his way to Madrid so quickly, perhaps not at all. But had he gone about his business in a slower, more laborious, more ordinary way, he might have been spared much pain.

Experts on foreign countries live in a state of perpetual uncertainty. They are supposed to know everything, and no one can know everything, or even very much, about a country. Soon in their career such experts indulge in little fraudulencies, then in greater ones, and finally in frightful lies. This predicament of the expert had long ago begun to affect the career of Professor Ratesby, and as his powers of impressive rhetoric developed, even to such an extent that he used them in ordinary conversation, so did his equally great powers of evasion. He could be inactive in a masterly way when he wished. In this instance he found that he did not want to continue investigations into the Society for the Promotion of Progressive International Contact. He had never heard of it. At the same time he was conscious of obligations to his friend. He satisfied his conscience by sending a telegram to Negrin, announcing the Canon's intended arrival, and another in the same sense, to the Society for the Promotion of Progressive International Contact.

The Canon was granted a visa on the strength of the first telegram, but no answer came from the second one. This, in the light of later events, should have caused the professor, and the Spanish Embassy, to inquire further, but they did not do so because they relied on each other excessively. When the party arrived in Barcelona, Ratesby was able to arrange for Symonston to accompany a liaison officer carrying despatches to the capital. At the end of these negotiations Ratesby felt pardonably proud of his success, and of his "not inconsiderable" influence. As for the Canon, he again felt grateful that he had such a friend. He left for Madrid. He felt so confident in the professor's powers that he paid no attention to the fact that no answer had even now been received from the Society in Madrid. He informed the secretary by telegram of the time of his arrival.

When they arrived at Madrid, the liaison officer left his charge abruptly. He had other more exciting interests, and he had done his job.

It was late afternoon. It was raining slightly. As he stood in the station the Canon was puzzled.

His rare journeys out of England had always confronted him with the expected: in Boulogne, in Italy, even in Russia, where he had visited a large match factory in which the beaming workers toiled to an accompaniment of beautiful and intricate community singing, he had found what he thought he would find. Madrid came as a mysterious shock. He had never been there before, and he had conceived but vague notions about it. He was prepared for a town looking rather like Venice. He had been able to see from the train that it was harsh, modern, and full of trams. He had supposed that he would find this Venetian scene desecrated by the horror of war; he imagined a Hades of screaming shells and echoing guns, terrible dashes to barricades, under the red flag. But instead he found uncanny normality, personified by the noise from outside of cars, whistles, and clanging tram bells. It was cold. He looked in every direction for a sign of the Society for the Promotion of Progressive International Contact. He showed his paper to a gendarme in a leather cocked hat, who merely shrugged his shoulders. He did the same to a friendly looking stranger, with the same negative result. No one had come to meet him.

He was wondering what to do next, whether to make

inquiries at the bank which was the Society's Head-quarters, when a man with his hands in his pockets, who had been watching him for a minute or so, walked up to him and addressed him in English:

"Excuse me," he said. "Aren't you Canon Symonston?"

"I am."

"I thought so. My name's Harry Elliot. I'm correspondent for the *Globe* out here. I saw your photograph in one of our North provincial papers once, and I've got a famous memory. You made a speech on something. Glad to meet you."

He was English, but he spoke with a slight trace of an American accent which he had picked up from American colleagues all over the world. He was large, rather untidily dressed, and his smile was expressive of reassuring good-fellowship. Like many journalists he was very much of an actor. You could see what he was from a long way off. He took great pride in his retentive memory. He acted his part conventionally.

"You are kind," said the Canon. He looked at him earnestly: "I hope you will not mind if I ask you for help. I am rather lost here."

"What can I do for you?"

"Well, I was expecting to be met, but as you see, I am alone. I am trying to find some people, that is to say, the people who invited me. What I really need is someone to put me in touch with the Society for the Promotion of Progressive International Contact, for they are the people in question. In Spanish — which I do not not speak — they are called — " and he produced his printed paper.

137

Elliot read the paper carefully.

"But don't you know these people?" he asked.

"Only from this one letter," and he produced the letter, rather in the style of one begging alms, and establishing the justice of his claims to charity. "We sent them a wire from Barcelona, but they do not seem to be here."

As Elliot read the paper and the letter, his face took on a gloomy look, and he shook his head. "I've never heard of them," he said, "and I know most of the Revolutionary clubs. I know all the important ones."

They looked at each other. The Canon was growing uneasy. He was grateful for Elliot's presence in this distant, strange land. Once more, as with Ratesby, he seemed fortunate in finding a protector.

"Look here," said Elliot, "we'd better ring them up. Come along with me." He picked up the Canon's two bags and they walked off to the public telephones which were near the station bar. He settled the Canon at a table with a cup of coffee and then went to the row of kiosks. He hunted for the Society in the directory, and, as he expected, he did not find it. He then took the Canon's letter, which he had with him, and from which he made out the surname of the secretary. He tried to find this name in the same volume. Hereon his luck improved, for at least he found it recorded, and at his first shot he struck near the target. He spoke to the secretary's aunt. She was alarmed and surprised by his inquiry, and more alarmed than surprised. She asked if Elliot was from the bank? Was young Ignacio in trouble? Why did the bank always want the address? She spoke high and shrilly. Elliot had such a pleasant way with him that his assurances that he was not speaking from the bank, that Ignacio was not in trouble, that, on the contrary, he was to be honoured by a visit from an admiring friend who had come all the way from England to see him, at last began to soothe her troubled mind. When he repeated that Ignacio had done nothing foolish or wrong, she gave him the address.

"Well, we've got the secretary's address," said Elliot, "let's push along and find him. He's got no phone."

"You are kind."

Elliot smiled. "It's all in the day's work," he said. This remark was more sincere than it sounded.

So the two set off together in a taxi for the secretary's house, which was situated in a poor quarter. It seemed now as though the problem was nearing solution, and yet, when they reached their goal, its dimensions grew rather than diminished. They found that the secretary, who lived in a minute garret at the top of a flight of dark stairs, was about seventeen years old. His astonishment at seeing the Canon was quite as great as their astonishment at seeing him.

Harry Elliot's mind worked mechanically, but never without imagination. Facts assembled in his head, and when enough were there, something like an instantaneous chemical process occurred. He then had a "story," and because he was a very good journalist indeed, the story was pretty near the truth as a rule. (Of course he had to earn his keep.) On this occasion he saw the story in one instant and satisfying flash. As soon as he saw the secretary, as soon as he saw his poor room, saw his untidy heap of books and papers, his squalor, his youth, his pride, he saw all.

"Now sit down, feller, and let's get this straight," he said, taking charge before the young man had time to recover from his shock. He sat on the bed, and the Canon followed him. He then questioned the secretary knowing well what the answers were likely to be, because the type of case was familiar to him.

This lad and his friends had met one evening and had been seized by a sudden impulse to save the world; and so there and then they formed the Society for the Promotion of Progressive International Contact. They had no money or influence, only burning beliefs. Among the latter was a conviction of the power of the printed word and it so happened that among this group was a young man who had a job in a printing works. Hence the manifesto. He had clandestinely set and printed it, without being found out. And the bank? This was the aunt's fault, although she was never consulted. She was the rich relative, which was why she had a telephone. She had her savings at the bank. They thought that the bank would give them prestige. (And were they not quite right?) And then — and then, oh, it was very plain from the secretary's embarrassment what had happened then. The report of the Canon's little speech in the newspaper appeared on that same day, and so they wrote to him, though why they selected him, and not one of the well-known and even extremer Leftists of England, was hard to say. When they had had no answer for more than ten

days, they began to see themselves as a set of rather foolish young men; their beliefs began to smoulder, not burn
as hitherto. They soon grew weary of disappointment:
the secretary stopped going to the bank, which was why
the bank rang up the aunt when the Canon's letter, and
later Ratesby's two telegrams, arrived. The Society had
entirely disintegrated.

And here was the Canon in person.

The young man, who at the beginning of Elliot's examination, was shy and nervous (for some time he and
his friends had been disturbed at the possibility that the
affair of the printing press might be discovered), now
began to turn his eyes on to the Canon with a look of
passion. The enormity of what had happened began to
present itself to his imagination. He felt like a table-
turner who has been answered by a personal manifestation, or an amateur chemist who suddenly discovers that
he is transforming lead into gold. His voice which had
been uncertain took on a new tone. "You must forgive
us for being unprepared," he cried to the Canon in tones
of thunder. "We will all reassemble this very night! Yes,
now! And tomorrow morning we will go to the Ministry
of War, and we will force them to give us a permit to go
to the front line. Yes! And when we are there we will
enrol! We will fight! We will kill! Ah, you give us in-
spiration for the struggle!"

"We are all in the struggle together, my child," said
the Canon with a melancholy smile.

Elliot, who was translating, broke in at this point.
"Look here, youngster," he said, "don't trouble about
tonight. I'll look after your friend now, and come and

141

see you here tomorrow around midday — that suit you? O.K. And don't worry — you're doing fine."

The two Englishmen left.

The next chapter of this history was devoted to a long search for accommodation. Madrid was crowded. It was now as they toured round the town in their taxi, visiting in vain every hotel and boarding house both rich and poor which Elliot knew; and as they grew miserably accustomed to the refrain that there was no room at the inn; it was now that the Canon began to see that in this town the misery of war lurked beneath the normal surface. He felt pity for the homeless, and he could not help including himself among them. He wondered what he would have done if he had not met Elliot by chance, and he felt grateful to him once more. As for Elliot, in the intervals between halts and arguments with porters and landladies, he was occupied with professional speculations. When he had first seen the Canon at the station he had felt a "hunch" that here was a story. He had been right, but unfortunately the story he had found was not of the kind for him. It would be easy to make fun of the secretary and his embarrassment, but this, besides being a cruel, reprehensible form of fun, was much too sophisticated fare for the *Globe*. So why was he wasting his time now? Human kindness? Yes, a little of that. Anything else? Well, yes, a lot. The "hunch" was still there. Given time, this obscure Leftist Canon in Madrid must make a story, the *Globe's* sort of story, and he was waiting for it to break. This angel of mercy was carnivorous.

Dusk was falling heavily. The rain still drizzled. No

room at the inn. It was nearly seven o'clock, and the situation was desperate.

"Look here, Canon," said Elliot, "if you don't mind roughing it, I believe I know of a place where I could get you a room. I'm thinking of a café near the Puerta de Sol. It's not a good hotel, but it's a hotel. It's our last chance, and if this fails — well, it's the floor of my flat. I'm sorry."

They went to the Hotel Flora.

From Elliot's warnings the Canon was expecting a scene of wretched squalor here, but he found instead exuberant modernistic jollity. Though it is true that much of the highly coloured paint was flaking off the walls, the large pillared hall was adorned with symbols of wealth. A frieze went round the upper wall showing semi-naked women dancing with castanets, and men in evening dress or national costume pursuing them, watching them, drinking champagne, kissing them on the lips. The hall was full of noise, of argument, laughter, and music. The place was packed with people sitting at tables. Over in the corner there was a high desk at which sat a fat dark scented jewelled lady. She was the proprietress. At her side stood a little elderly man, her husband. Elliot set the Canon down on a chair by a table and approached this couple. He laid a hand on the fat lady's arm.

"Now look," he said, "you've got to help me because I'm in a jam. I've got to have a room."

She gave him an arch maternal smile. "For you, Señor Elliot, I always have a room. You know the terms."

"Yes, but that's just it, Ma Valdés, I don't want it for myself. I want it for my friend, the fellow sitting down over there with the priest's collar on. He'll give you no trouble."

Señora Valdés was not a narrow-minded woman, as the reader may have guessed, but she firmly drew the line at anything in the nature of what she termed "funny business" being conducted on the premises. She looked at Elliot now with an expression less maternal than hitherto. "Now look here," she said, "just why are you so interested in getting a room for a priest, eh?"

"Don't always jump to conclusions, Ma Valdés. He's English, he's a sort of relative of mine, an uncle — you know."

"Yes," she said, "*I* know those sort of uncles." She put up her pince-nez spectacles and looked at the Canon.

The latter was feeling wholly lost, more lost than he had felt in his life before, even since his arrival in Madrid that afternoon. His mind was a blank. The noise of this place confused him. In a sort of dream he saw Elliot arguing at the desk with the fat painted woman and her husband, saw her look at him angrily, and Elliot leaning forward and speaking earnestly in a low voice. He saw numerous people come into the overlit and garish hall, and leave it by the loudly slamming swing door. At the tables men and women were drinking and laughing, many of the women sitting on the knees of the men. They kissed and bellowed and screamed. He heard the din of a mechanical piano coming through a half-open door. And all this he but little comprehended. He dimly realized that these were the people whom he had come to succour, to pay homage to, to fortify. He was very tired.

Over in the corner the argument was going forward. "Now do see sense, Ma Valdés. This guy isn't going to cause you any worry. He's not going to bring down the reputation of the house. He's not a Renegade. He's just got to have somewhere to doss down till we've had time to regulate his position as a guest of the country with the Ministry of Foreign Affairs."

It was now that the husband joined in. "Did you say he will be a guest of the Government?" he asked.

"That's right."

"And did you say one night only?"

"Yes. One night. That's all."

He tapped his wife on the arm. "Beloved one," he said, "suppose we were to say that this old man is the guest of the Government now, and that our rooms are requisitioned for him. Is that not a convenient mode of ridding the house of the two gipsies?" She turned and looked at him, for a moment quite bewildered with admiration. "Oh, we lose a little, of course," he said, "but we can rent the room for as much the day after, and we are spared the — esāndalo — the scandal!" He uttered the last word in fierce anger.

"Señor Elliot," said Señora Valdés, after a little further conference with her husband, "listen to this proposition. Your friend may have a room for one night, for one night only, but only on condition that you help us as I ask. It is like this: there are two women here and they share a room. We call them gipsies. That," she explained,

145

"is because they are not serious." And she pursed her lips and looked at him with a formidable expression. "They make noise, they break things, they bring undesirable persons to the house. Two in one room are always bad like that; indeed we were foolish to take them. We have tried to rid ourselves of them, but their friends are violent, uncontrollable; they threaten us. They have threatened to hurl my husband down into the courtyard from above when he has protested against the misconduct of those two and their companions. Now, Señor Elliot, if you will get them out of their room you can have it for your friend. You will say you have come to us from the British Embassy. You will say that the Ministry has authorized the Embassy to commandeer one room from us. We are sorry, of course, but what can we do if the Ministry and the Embassy insist." She threw up her hands. Then she looked at him with a merry light in her eyes. "That is how you can get the room."

"But really," said Elliot, "you know our Embassy can't do that, and even if they could, I don't belong to the damned thing. Why can't you do it?" he asked of the husband.

The proprietress leaned towards her husband, putting her protective bulk between the two men. She said: "I have told you how you can get the room. No other way. Do what you want."

Elliot scratched his head.

"Have these two girls anywhere to go if I turn them out?"

"Have they got . . . Ha! Ha! Ha! My God!"

"Oh, all right, then. I'll do it."

The Canon was in difficulties as a blond young German had joined him at his table and given him a brandy and soda.

"You priest," said his companion. "All priest in Spain bad. They bad mens. All priest in Germany good mens. Good, good, good. Good like me. Mr. Hitler persecute against." He shouted to make himself heard over the thunder of the mechanical piano.

"We are international," smiled the Canon.

"International not good. International bourgeois bad bloody ting. Fight."

"Remember the *Third* International," said the Canon.

But the Teuton, in the manner of his race, maintained a steady concentration on the original subject. "In world cataclysmus was international banker, und international priest, und international bourgeois militar join up to make war on people. Wherefore in Schpain priest bad ting." As though to mark the conclusion of the argument he leaned forward and glowered into the Canon's face.

"We are at cross purposes," smiled the Canon.

The German made the motions of firing a machine-gun. "Shoot off bourgeois people then better."

The Canon's attention was drawn to Elliot, whom he saw on the stairs with two young women, a fair one and a dark one. Elliot was behind the two women, carrying their bags, and trying to make the downward pace in the style of a man driving geese down a hill. As with geese, the descent was not continuous, but broken at every five or six steps by incident, by first one and then the other turning and screaming at Elliot in a torrent of angry language; by an effort to break through and past him; by

147

the fair one suddenly sitting down, looking haughtily
away from Elliot, while he, guarding the way against
another upward dash, distributed some money to both;
by other emotional episodes in which tears and giggles
were mingled. From the distance of the stairs they looked
beautiful. When they came closer the Canon remarked
that the lovely golden hair of one was streaked with
dark brown, that her teeth were decayed, and that she
had a pock-marked skin overladen with coarse paint; and
that the darker one was hirsute, gold-toothed, and pock-
marked too. He watched their slow progress to the desk;
saw the proprietress throw up her hands as though in
despair; heard them scream in unison so loud that even
in this babel the noise arrested people's attention; saw
Elliot produce a bank note, hold it up and make a sort
of oration over it, in the middle of which it was snatched
from his hand by one of them. And then they left
quickly. The Canon saw and heard all this, understanding nothing, while at the same time attempting to listen
politely to the German. Elliot came over.

"Well, that's fixed, Canon," he said, and turned to
order some more brandy from a waiter. "It's not a good
hotel, but as I said it's a hotel. A bit noisy. Buzz off,
Hans." This was to the German, who left obediently.
"You've got a room which the old girl there'll show you,
and they produce quite a decent meal in that big hall over
there. You can stay here tonight, and tomorrow we'll
get you fixed up properly as a guest of the Ministry."
And he gave him a queer look, uncertain whether he
ought to explain candidly just what sort of a hotel this

was. The waiter came up with drinks on a tray. He decided he had said enough. "Well, here's how," he said.

"You have done wonders," replied the Canon, "I am most awfully grateful to you. You have been really a friend in need." He drank his brandy.

"I'll see you in the morning and fix for you to meet someone. Good night." Elliot left.

It was after eight, and the Canon was in his room. He was well pleased with it, although, in a time of overcrowding, he would have preferred to have been given a room with only one bed in it. But war is the season of infectious selfishness, and his Christian scruples struggled against his delight at finding, after his sleepless night in the train, and his agonizing search, this pleasing yielding softness. He was enjoying a brief rest before dinner. He had washed his face and hands, and washing was no small joy either. He lay, clothed only in his shirt, trousers, and socks, in the bliss of a soft bed. How great are the daily pleasures of the world!

He was suffered to remain thus happy for fifteen minutes, when there was a knock. He roused himself with a little groan of disappointment, and getting up, and slightly opening the door, he looked out. He found about seven men, standing in the corridor. For a moment there was silence while they looked at each other. Then one of the seven said something in a good-humoured tone in Spanish. The Canon tried to reply in a suitable fashion.

"Señor Symonston. English. Inglés," he said.

The effect of this speech was disappointing. No eluci-
dation followed from the other side. Smiling, with his
head on one side, one of the men began to say something in a half-humorous, half-persuasive sing-song tone.
Another, who was leaning against the opposite wall with
his hands in his pockets, said in English: "All right. All
right." Then the first speaker, having pointed to the in-
terior of the room stretched out his hand and closed the
door. The Canon returned to his bed in renewed bewilderment. He had quite enough bewilderment for one
day.

As he lay resting again his thoughts on this seemingly
senseless interruption were formless. If a man had mistaken the number of his room, that would be understandable; the inexplicable thing was the fact of the in-
truders being so many: seven at the least. And then, from
the thought of their numbers, with a sudden thrill, he
realized what it all meant. Of course! These must be
the people who, of all people, should have been uppermost in his mind: this clearly was a deputation from the
Society for the Promotion of Progressive International
Contact. Elliot, of course, must have informed the young
secretary about where their guest was staying, and with
that courtesy for which he believed Spaniards were famous, they had immediately sent round a Welcome Committee. And he had as good as turned them away! Oh,
dear, how ungracious they must think him, and how
ungrateful. But was it too late? Perhaps they were still
in the hotel, in the hall no doubt. Should he go down?
Yes, he must. He would. And so, rising once more from
his bed, he went to the dressing-table, brushed his hair

and put on his shoes. But before he had finished there was a second knock at his door, but this time it was a loud rude rap, and it was followed by the sound of voices. The Canon remembered that the Spaniards were reputed to be violent as well as courteous. Well, at all events, there was no doubt about it now. He was clearly the object of their search.

He opened the door and walked out into the passage. He was greeted by a savage tumult of voices over which the English speaking one shouted: "All right. All right," in anger. The Canon raised his hand.

"My friends," he said, "I know no Spanish. You perhaps will help me?" He indicated the Angloloquent, who replied: "All right."

"Our friend will tell you what I say," went on the Canon, nodding to the interpreter. "First let me say how glad I am to see you all. Thank you for your invitation. Thank you. I have long looked forward to this moment. The struggle in Spain is the struggle of us all." Here the Canon paused. He believed that he was succeeding. The frowning, ardent passionate looks of these men, and the queer squeezed-up features of the interpreter who had throughout kept up a passionate mutter, allowed him to believe that his words were somehow reaching his audience. "In Spain the struggle has broken out in battle, and war, and violence. So be it. At the other end of the world the same thing came to pass. I have been to Russia." He paused and his impression that somehow — incredibly — his improvised oratory had moved them, grew stronger. A man, who till now had been asleep on a chair in the corridor, woke and stood up looking about him, swaying strangely. "Yes, I have been to Russia. I have seen your cause, I have seen our cause, every one's cause, the cause of the world, I have seen it . . . triumphant!"

At this moment there occurred an annoying anti-climax. The interpreter barged his way through the audience, and, hands in pocket still, barged his way past the speaker into the bedroom, while the members of the deputation all began to speak at once. Canon Symonston was about to resume, when the interpreter barged back again out of the room, and spoke to the rest of them. And when they had heard him they shrugged their shoulders and talking volubly turned round and began to walk away, as though having suddenly lost all interest. The interpreter laid a hand on the Canon's shoulder and said amid much lingering garlic and alcohol: "All right. No good. All right," and walked away with the rest. The bewildered Canon saw that the sleeper whom he had awakened was once more in his chair with his head nodding forward on his breast. He was left alone. Evidently he had not been understood after all.

He returned to his room too agitated for sleep. It was getting on for a quarter to nine. He decided to dress completely and go downstairs for an evening meal. When he was ready, and had washed afresh, and brushed his hair, he sat down, suddenly overcome by the utter strangeness of what he had been through. Here he was in the midst of a terrible war. . . . He sat thus pondering for several minutes.

For the third time there was a knock at his door. But this time it was terrifically loud and accompanied by a heavy kick and a roar. For the third time the Canon went to the door but before he had time to turn the knob it was flung open by a middle-aged man dressed in military uniform, evidently of high rank, and he recognized him, even in that moment of palsying fear, as the man who had been asleep on a chair in the corridor. Like a tiger this man flung himself into the room howling words which, if he had understood Spanish, would have meant to the Canon: "Enough! Enough! Where is she? Son of a bitch! You have hidden her! Goat! Out of my way!" He rushed at the Canon and sent him crashing to the far side of the room, overturning the dressing-table by the window. Then he tore open the cupboard. He threw himself into it, and frothed among the priest's garments, then staggered back out of it, to the bed over which he backwards tottered, and began grasping madly for the pistol in his holster. The fact that this Colonel, tossed on the springs of the mattress, rolled horribly on to the floor, gave Symonston time to open the window, see where the fire-escape was, and make for it quickly.

I have already told what remains of this story.

The person who suffered most was Elliot who, as I mentioned earlier, had felt throughout that the Canon would ultimately lead him to a great story. He made all the right moves, but without success. As soon as he knew of the accident and had interviewed the Canon, he went in search of the gipsies whose address he had not much difficulty in finding from Señora Valdés. But they were so terrified by what they had heard that they could only scream that they were innocent. For their own sakes and that of their friend they kept from him not only the name of the Colonel, but the fact that they knew him, and so he missed the connection between him and them and the assault. But much later when the whole affair was becoming distant and forgotten, he met these two women again, by chance, in a bar, and he stood them drinks. It was then that he learned the real facts from the golden-haired one, and though he had had much success with the story of the Fifth Columnist, the truth affected him with a feeling of bitter frustration. He was an artist, and he liked accuracy. "If only I had known at the time," he moaned.

But she said: "It is a great thing to be loved by a man with such passion."

✣ Not for Psychologists

THE CONGO is a great and beautiful river. That much is easily said, but it is difficult to describe in more detail, and at the same time in a vivid manner, the spectacle of this mass of moving water, and the dark jungles through which it passes, because some of the splendour of the scene lies in the fact that its beauty is of a known and obvious kind. The Congo is not one of those phenomena of nature which impress upon you the mystery of real presence, which make one exclaim: "Oh, I could never have guessed this!" No, for all its vastness and wonder, it is entirely guessable. People sometimes talk as though Equatorial Africa were now no longer a wild land, as though the days of hacked-out pathways, of constant danger from the great beasts, of dark forest and jungle untrod by the foot of man, belong to the past, and that the whole thing is now neatly tamed. But the more traditional view is the correct one. As you fly in an aeroplane over that place you see a landscape of thick forest broken only by rocky mountains, and cloven by the mile-wide river after which part of it is named. At very rare intervals indeed you notice what look like little patches by the shore scratched bare. The aeroplane begins to circle and lower: these little bare patches are famous colonial cities: Stanleyville, Nouvelle Anvers, Coquilhatville, Leopoldville.

They are agreeable towns, clean and well-ordered, and the Belgians have succeeded in introducing many comforts of their civilized life into these fierce hostile regions. In the hotels you can get good French meals, good wine to drink, and if you stay in the lounge you might suppose yourself in a hot Europe. But if you go out, there, instantly before you, is nature in her most dreadful majesty. I called the river mile-wide, but it is often much more than that: the farther shore is sometimes so distant that you have the impression of being at the side of a lake. Near to the shore, plying hither and thither, you see native boats manned by blacks, carrying merchandise and sometimes conveying a person of note who sits proudly in the bows. Huge and lovely flowers grow everywhere, and they glitter against the dark green of the forest. Often the sight of a wonderful, brightly-coloured bird takes you by surprise, and quite often too you feel that peculiar thrill of horror which we experience at the sight of some large and unfamiliar insect.

I have only once been to the Congo, and then, strangely enough, was given a free trip by air all the way from Upper Egypt to the Atlantic because I was not important enough to be sent home from Cairo more cheaply. This may sound a little mad, so let me explain. In our planned age there are things called "priorities," and, in the war, the system of priorities was applied to the transport of military personnel. Thus, for example, in Cairo, if you were above the rank of Colonel, or were engaged on an urgent mission, you were given "Priority A" when you needed to go on a long journey. This meant that you went the quickest way. If you were bound for England it meant you made a swift, fatiguing, and not very interesting journey by French North Africa and Gibraltar. If you were less than a Colonel, and not very vital to victory, you were given "Priority B" or "C." To reach England you then made a long, delightful, and instructive journey round Upper Egypt, Central Africa, Portugal and Ireland, the kind of "Rundfahrt" only undertaken by adventurous millionaires in times of peace; and yet such is the power of snobbishness in the world that men would go to formidable lengths of intrigue to be accounted "Priority A," and to avoid this longer route which, for all its glamour and beauty, did mean, in the words of an expressive vulgarism, that you were not "out of the top drawer." Oh, but there was more in it than that. The Congo route set a mark upon you which needed explaining away. People who made a mess of their missions, or who had bungled their commands, or who were facing grave charges, went home by these equatorial lands. To be seen leaving Cairo that way, if you held senior rank, was like being seen entering the Tower, in days gone by, through Traitor's Gate. Of course, it didn't necessarily mean anything — but all the same . . .

My own case was innocent and typical. I belonged to a mission which had finished its work, and I was sent home to England for re-employment. I was given "Priority C." I was a straight plain instance of inferiority, of be-longing to the lower classes of State service, of not hail-

ing from top-drawers but from larger, more squalid re-
ceptacles. So it came about that one day in the Spring
of 1943, I was placed on a flying-boat on the Nile and
sent up to Khartoum, our first stage, with some twenty
other untouchables.

Three days later, we were in Stanleyville. On the
morning after our arrival we were told that there was a
report of bad weather ahead of us, and so we would have
to remain where we were till the next day. We had made
friends with each other by now, and in our weak human
fashion were beginning to form cliques. My own chosen
crony was a handsome young Colonel of somewhat
Jewish appearance, though fair in colour, and with
pleasant smooth manners. His name was Walshe. Unlike most of the others he seemed pleased that we were
delayed.

"This will give me the chance to look at a black village
or two," he said.

The Belgian authorities were anxious that we should
receive a good impression of their great colony, and soon
after the meteorological officer had told us that we could
not go on, two ladies appeared and announced their
intention of organizing diversions to relieve our tedium.
There was a beautiful country club nearby, with tennis
courts and a swimming pool, and the two ladies described
in their broken English how they intended to take us for
a drive, and then to the club. This would fill up the
morning. The afternoon would be spent asleep, and in
the evening they would arrange for a film to be shown
in the hotel. They made these plans with the senior
member of our party, an Air Commodore.

"I think that sounds capital," he said. "Thanks very much indeed." He then turned to *his* crony, a young Group Captain, and said in a loud voice: "Since we've got to stop might as well enjoy ourselves. I sent my Number Two home on my priority A as he's a specialized photographic interpreter — but I must say I'd have thought twice if I'd known we were liable to be held up. Still there we are. Ha, ha, ha."

Colonel Walshe was eyeing one of the ladies. He drew her aside from the throng which we all formed, and spoke to her alone for a little time. Then he came to me.

"Look, I've arranged a car for myself, and a guide, to go to a black village. Will you come with me?"

"Yes, I'd like that."

We made our arrangements with conspiratorial hush, as we did not want the others to know what we intended. We felt that a black village would be best observed without the intrusion of a crowd. We hid in the deserted bar to await our guide. Soon the others left.

The black village was about twenty miles away and was almost the size of a small town. There was something strangely exciting in seeing people as primitive as its population, and as different in race from ourselves; in watching the jerky yet beautiful rhythm of their walk, and the look of fear with which some of them peered at us from their hovels. I felt moved to an indefinable emotion, like pity, by the childish way these tall and beautiful human beings tried to overcome their shyness of us. We spoke to them through our guide, as much as we could, but it was almost impossible for people as inexperienced as we to make any sensible contact with them. They were much too panicky. Walshe did more talking than I did; he was more pertinacious, but equally unsuccessful. I noticed the rank and not disagreeable smell which came from their glistening bodies. The heat was easily borne as the dampness made us sweat the whole time. Walshe and I walked round the village looking like two actors in an old-fashioned film.

When we had seen half, Walshe said to me: "This guide is pretty useless. I want to see the witch-doctor here and he goes on telling me there isn't one."

"Perhaps there isn't."

"But there certainly is. Did you see a man with a stiff arm in that crowd I was trying to talk to just now?"

I remembered that in a heap of chattering black bodies sitting by a stream washing their clothes and linen, there had been a man whose arm seemed paralysed and was held in an odd position.

"Yes. What of him?"

"Did you notice that the arm looked perfectly normal — I mean not deformed in any way at all?"

"I noticed no deformity. Why?"

"Well, this guide heard from the people that his arm is like that because of a curse. He struck his father and as a punishment the witch-doctor cursed his arm and he can't move it. I want to meet that witch-doctor. I want to know how the devil he does it. He must be a genius the size of Mesmer; he must be the greatest hypnotist of all time; or else he really is a magician."

I turned to the guide: "Ici dans le village, il y a un sorcier, n'est-ce pas?"

"Blait-il?"

"Un sorcier, magicien, un prêtre — what are they called in French?"

"I don't know. Un homme spirituel. No, that's no good. Un sorcier, you know, un sorcier."

"Na, Manseer. Bas de sorciers. Na. Na."

"Mais vous avez dit à moi," went on Walshe. "Rapellez l'homme avec le mauvais bras. Les gens ont dit et vous avez repété à moi. Un sorcier, ils ont dit."

"Ce pupple très ignorang, manseer. Très sumple. Ce qu'ils dire," he rolled his eyes and made gestures with his hands over his lips, "ce n'est pas bong. Ils n'avoir pas d'educationg, manseer. Sorcier est ridicool."

"O oui, je sais, ça c'est très possible. Je ne contradicte pas vous. Mais tout de même je veux interviewer le sorcier. Je n'objecte pas même s'il est ridicule. Où est-il?"

"Na! Na! Manseer, bas de sorciers. En tout bays Cango Belge bas. Sorcier mauvais. Sorcier va. Pouf! Pouf!" It was evident that our guide was against witch doctors, but it was difficult to tell whether he really regarded them as ridiculous, or as objects of fear.

"That's not what he said before," Walshe muttered angrily. "He told me that this man had been paralysed for a year owing to a curse. Even if he's exaggerating fantastically — even if he means only a month, it's incredible! Voyez," he went on, making a last hopeless attempt, "Je ne suis pas an agent de votre Gouvernement. Je promesse de ne reporter pas le sorcier. Je veux seulement demander de lui comment il fait ça. Seulement pour mon interesse."

But the guide only said again: "Na, manseer, bas de sorcier."

We went over the rest of the village, saw what domestic animals they kept, entered some of their houses, tasted some of their food, and by a stroke of luck saw a chieftain in what looked to me like ceremonial dress, a tall dignified figure carrying a spear, naked except for a short brilliantly-coloured cloak and two bright feathers in his hair, and beads and metal bracelets on his magnificent muscular arms, followed by a henchman carrying a shield and two other spears. They looked like figures on a Greek urn. I found the whole scene wonderful, but Walshe took little pleasure in it. His morning's expedition had been made miserable by his failure over the witch-doctor, and nothing could cheer him. When he was not silent he was nagging at the guide to take him to see the object of his curiosity, and the guide nagged back that no such man existed. He looked wretchedly gloomy as we drove back to the country club, and I wondered whether my new-found friend was going to turn out to be a tediously moody man.

In the evening, after the five-minute sunset, when we were all sitting at tables on the little piazza in front of the hotel, and the Group Captain was loudly and mirthfully telling of the odd circumstances in which *he* had been given a "Priority B," Walshe and I came together again for a glass of gin before dinner. We watched the unfamiliar constellations: the Southern Cross, the False Cross, the Ship, the Scorpion, and the Great Bear lying on his back for a change. After a long pause in our talk, he said: "Sickening about that witch-doctor."

"But why are you so interested in him?"

"Because I'm one myself. I wanted to compare notes."

"Indeed? You surprise me." He smiled, enjoying his joke, till a look of seriousness followed suddenly.

"Yes, it's true. That was the reason at the back of my mind when I asked for this passage. I ought strictly to have gone the other way. I've got a 'Priority A.' No one else has here, I'll be bound. The point is I wanted to see something of black people, and their customs, and reactions, and behaviour, and so on. It's a thing I've missed through taking up practice too early. But of course I never expected to get such a prize exhibit as a witch-doctor. And then I do get this perfect gift — only to have it instantly snatched away. *Maddening!*"

"What is your job exactly? You aren't medical, surely?" He was not wearing the crimson tabs of the medical service, but ordinary scarlet ones. I had assumed that he was an Intelligence Officer.

"Not exactly," said Walshe. "I'm semi-medical, semi-Intelligence. In private life I'm a psychiatrist. I've been in Mid-East to make a psychological study of the Eighth Army."

"Shell-shock? That sort of thing?"

"No. Morale is my great subject. State of mind of the men."

"Is it good?"

"Yes. Pretty well the same as in any army capable of giving battle. Not much hysteria — not much panic, as you'd say — which is the main thing. Oh yes, it's all right. My report didn't reach your office in GHQ? "

"No. Was it interesting?"

His Jewish ancestry showed in the delicate way he raised his shoulders and spread out his hands with a gentle touch of mockery in his exaggeration. "They wanted to know how the men were feeling, and so, after a few hundred interviews, and watching correspondence, I told them."

"And what do the men feel?"

"When the situation is dangerous they feel frightened. When it becomes less dangerous they feel less frightened. They feel more frightened in the front line than in the rear. They are perturbed by the possibility of sudden death. Scenes of carnage shake their nerves. They quell these feelings of fear by the wilful exercise of courage. They hope we win the war. That's what I discovered."

"Remarkable. Anything else?"

"Indeed. Being away from home makes them melancholy. They feel homesick. They look forward to returning to their homes, except for a few. They — the majority I mean — hope this wish is soon realized."

"And were the authorities impressed by your discoveries?"

"Very. They really were. Perhaps because I'm travelling home on a 'Priority B' route you don't believe that I am in good faith. But I have an 'A' voucher in my pocket. Of course, I wrote my report in highly technical terms. I may even get promotion."

"But — but what did they like about your discoveries — I mean, so very much?"

"We live in an age of science, and I was able to prove scientifically certain facts. That these facts are so obvious that anyone except a half-wit might guess them is not important. The thing is they are preoccupations, and it is inestimably important for those in authority to have besetting preoccupations described in learned language. This enables the authorities to look at them calmly. It gives them confidence and makes them better at their jobs. They feel that their problems are now under control."

"But are they? Could you offer any remedies for this fear and homesickness?"

"Naturally. The homesickness is cured by sending them home, the fear by removing the danger."

"I don't know what we'd do without you."

At this he looked serious again, and I thought, for a moment, that my facetious remark might have sounded offensive. But he was not offended, he was serious because he was interested.

"We are good scientists on the whole," he said, "but the people who consult us are not. We can find out almost anything, but as for putting it straight — "

"You mean that if I develop some mania, you can tell what it is, but you cannot help me to get rid of it."

"Oh, no. That is much too wide a generalization. Psychologists have restored shattered people to complete sanity quite often, but, in my own opinion, this positive, or you could even say this creative activity, has nothing much to do with the science we profess. It has to do with the man in charge at the moment. If he is a man of compelling, beautiful or peculiarly charming character, why then, he can use the immense influence psychiatry gives him to achieve miracles of transformation. It's been done. But does psychiatry mean intensity or goodness of character? Of course it doesn't. A most unscientific idea."

He laughed to himself and offered me a cigarette. It was still hot and we were sweating. The descent of the sun had made no perceptible difference to the temperature. Moths fluttered round the lamps in clouds, and occasionally a dragon-fly darted into them with a whizz.

I said: "Here is an idea which has often occurred to me. Most people, so it seems, who consult psychiatrists are extraordinarily weak-willed. They are in a vicious circle; weakness caused their trouble and only innate strength, which they haven't got, can pull them out. Am I right?"

He nodded. "Near enough, in some cases."

"Now, here's the rest of the idea. Surely psychiatry must be a quite different thing when you are dealing with a man who has the natural degree of strength of mind. I'm thinking of the case of a man of ordinary character, a basically normal man, who has met with a psychological accident. You must have come across many such among your shell-shock cases. Surely you can cure them easily enough?"

"That's a very well-worn notion," he said, "but no use. Basic normality is a fiction. The human mind is a fearful contraption, a mass of wild impulse, just kept in a reasonable position by delicately organized stresses and counter-stresses. The real marvel of psychology is that the balance should be so generally maintained, considering how it can be destroyed by little things. I used to half-believe in 'basic normality' from habit (because we don't much hold with it in our teaching), until what looked like a basically normal man came to me for help one day. He turned out to be my most perfect failure.

He is on my mind to-day. I'd have given anything to have met that witch-doctor."

"So you're back to the witch-doctor. I'd almost forgotten him. Why does *he* interest you so much?"

"Because, by means which I can hardly imagine, he did what I once tried to undo. He is the hero of my story. What a pity he wasn't there at the time!"

"What story?"

"I've told you the end of it. Do you want the beginning?"

"Is it interesting?"

"Not for psychologists. It might be for you."

Before 1939 Henry Walshe was well-known for his skill in psychiatry. He had a large practice, and if his reputation was somewhat exaggerated this was due not to himself but to many of his women patients. One day, to his surprise, he was approached by Mr. George Berrington whose wife's ills he had diagnosed in the course of many interviews. Berrington rang him up and asked if he could see him on an urgent matter that day.

Berrington was a large red-faced, middle-aged man, with a square nose and a protruding upper lip, considerably his wife's senior. He was badly and expensively dressed in a brown double-breasted suit, black shoes with grey spats, and a tie with purple, green, and blue stripes in the pattern. He seemed very much embarrassed at finding himself in Walshe's consulting-room, and it was not difficult to guess that he had passed through some degree of mental struggle before making his appointment. As with our black guide and the witch-doctoring, he seemed uncertain whether to treat this form of hocus-pocus with contempt or terror. Walshe gave him a cigarette, placed him in a comfortable chair, asked after his wife, and then suggested that he should tell him what troubled him.

"Well," he began — he spoke with a thick Midlands accent, "it's not for meself, you know. It's about one of my men. It's rather peculiar, you know; I mean it's such an odd sort of case that I don't quite know what you'll make of it."

Walshe smiled with a well-practised show of good nature. "I'm very used to odd cases," he said, "and while I don't know if I can help until you've told me, I don't think you will surprise me. Tell me about it. Don't hold anything back — that's the important thing. Tell me in your own way."

At this encouragement Berrington looked up with a dog-like expression of gratitude and gave a whistling sigh of relief. He looked at his cigarette, darted his little eyes at Walshe again, and then began: "I don't know how much you know about me. I'm a business man. I come from Sheffield. I'm in a Light Steel works there: Bowker, Coutts, and Berrington; you may know the name. We've a fair-sized workshop even by Sheffield standards; there aren't many to come up to us, and last year our turn-over was right up in the quarter million class. Now, as you'd imagine, our machinery takes a lot of looking after, and I can't be too careful who I get as my foremen. They've got to be highly-graded specialists who can spot an error a mile away and take a big machine to pieces and put it together again with their eyes shut;

168

and they've got to know how to manage men, and be on the right side of the Union, too. They're not easily found, those fellows, and when you've got one you want to keep 'im. And if you pick a dud, Dr. Walshe, then you're landed with him for life, because you can't get rid of him these days like you could do. No, believe me, senior foremen are a big problem in a works like ours.

"Well, now, I'll tell you what's worrying me. My best foreman is a man called Whitfield, a Sheffield man. I've known him and his family ever since he was a kid, because his father, and his grandfather too, worked for Coutts in the old days. That man's been brought up alongside machinery since ever he could walk. He's still young, not over forty, and we've had our eye on him for some time as our next works engineer-manager. I like the man too and I'd do a lot rather than get rid of Whitfield." He paused and looked defiantly at the psychiatrist, as though he had said something rather shocking.

"But why should you get rid of him?"

Berrington gave his head a sideways toss. "I'm going to tell you. Listen to this. Whitfield's got something wrong with his arm. Nothing much because he can use it to the full whenever he wants, and he's a strong man and works hard with his hands. But he's got some sort of rheumatics. That's what the doctors say. His right arm's for ever aching. Not badly, mark you, not so as to make him a regular martyr, but there's this rheumatic pain for ever in his arm. I sent him up to Harrogate last year, and he came back as right as rain, but then, after a week or two here's this pain back again in his arm. He's been to a specialist on rheumatism in Sheffield, tip-top chap, and he can't do anything with him either. It's the same thing always, he gets right for a week, and then there's the pain back again. Now I'm going to tell you something rather queer. Before we found out about the rheumatics we thought he'd permanently injured his arm in an accident. That was a natural thing to think, because, you see it so happened that a little time after he'd first come to us — near fifteen years ago — he had an accident. He got his arm, his right arm, the same one, caught in a fly-wheel and wrenched good and proper. He'd have been killed for certain, or lost his arm, if there hadn't been a man right by the engine who pulled him out quick as lightning. As it was he was disabled for a month, but the arm got all right again. It's been looked at thoroughly. It's been X-rayed and they say there's nothing wrong, no permanent injury. Of course a lot of people say the doctors don't know their job and the arm is still injured from the accident. So you might think, but I happen to know better. Whitfield's told me himself, and in confidence, that he had the rheumatics in his arm long before the accident. But I want you to keep that to yourself, and you'll see why in a minute."

"It is a rule that what you say here is told to no one unless you wish it."

"Wuh? Oh, yes, I suppose so. No offence, I trust." Berrington blushed heavily.

"No. Go on about Whitfield. Did he have another accident?"

Berrington stared at him. "Why yes, he did," he said faintly, continuing to stare, overcome for a moment by Walshe's unearthly insight.

There was a pause, and then, after an audible gulp, he continued: "Just a matter of three weeks ago. Horrible accident, and just like the first one, but again saved in the nick o' time, and not such a bad wrench. He was only disabled for a few days. Of course the board weren't pleased, and as I look after the workshop side I told them I'm going to talk to Whitfield sharply and give him warning. I had him up in my office a week later. 'Arm all right now?' I say.

" 'Yes, Sir,' he says. 'Out of a sling two days.'

" 'I'm glad to hear it,' I says. 'But look here, Whitfield,' I says, 'I've got to talk to you seriously about these accidents because it's happened before, and the board aren't pleased about it, and no more am I. A man of your experience getting his hand into a fly — why it's a disgrace. It's just downright careless. And I'm warning you, Whitfield, that it's not escaped notice. You want to look sharp.'

"He looks very shaken by what I say, so I speaks to him a bit more kindly. 'I can't understand it,' I say, 'because it isn't as if you was a careless man. It isn't as if you're a man I could complain of in a general way. Why, you're about our best engineer, and you know it. And then — twice — you go and do a damn-fool thing like that, and for no reason. Not as if the engine had been out of order. Not as if you was acting in an emergency. What came over you?'

"Those last words of mine fairly knocked him up. He just dropped into a chair, a thing he'd never do ordinary, and looks as if he's going to pass out. 'Mr. Berrington,' he says, 'I'm a wash-out. You'd better get rid of me.' I

171

say to him: 'Oh, come now, Whitfield, you're not a touchy bloke. Pull yourself together, man.' But he just sits there and looks as if he's going to faint. White as a sheet, and shaking all over. I keep a spot o' whisky in my office, and he looks as if he needs it, so I give him a nip. And then he perks up a bit and talks. 'It's my arm,' he says. 'It's this arm' . . . He tells me he's had this pain in his arm ever since he was a young man and left the army in 1920. It's not a bad pain, he says, nothing to worry about, hardly notices it. But he says when he had his accidents his arm hurt him a lot — just before they happened. The pain suddenly come on, he says, and then he has a blackout, and the next thing he knows he's lying on the floor with the men all round him and his arm nearly wrenched off. He says it happened just the same both times. No memory of the accident itself — just a blackout. I'm a bit shaken myself when I hear this. It's so queer, I mean. And when he says, 'That's how it is, Mr. Berrington. You can't keep me on when I might do it again any time' — why I don't know how to answer him. I'm just worried to death about the whole thing. It's so queer. You see it isn't as though he's funny in the head. He's as sane as I am. And one night I tell Mavis, and Mavis says, 'Oh, you go to Harry Walshe,' she says, 'he knows all about cases like that,' and we talk it over. So she persuades me to come along and see you. That's the whole story, Dr. Walshe. What do you make of it?"

"Nothing yet. I must know a lot more about this man."

Whitfield was a small stocky fellow, with a snub nose, and round yet bony face. In everything he was very typical of a Midland plebeian: in his pale skin and dark hair, in his expression of obstinacy and determination, in his quiet manners, in his solitary piece of dandyism: a quiff of hair trained to roll up from his forehead. As he stood in his neat blue suit in Walshe's consulting room, a week after Berrington's visit, he looked the very image of common sense, as though he was made of that and nothing more.

Walshe had concluded his first examination of him, not very satisfactorily, because, since Whitfield was a man of very limited education, his mind grew stiff and awkward in the presence of what was new to him. There was a natural impulse of rejection with which he responded to the unfamiliar notion of deep analysis, so much so that Walshe saw that he must decide between a very lengthy examination, a process which would wear down Whitfield's unwilled resistance; and the use of hypnosis. He was inclined towards the latter, because he knew how well people of stubborn character usually react to hypnosis once consent has been fully given. Here, however, Walshe met a new and unexpected complication. Whitfield's meagre reading had unfortunately included the classic fiction on that mysterious subject.

Whitfield stood silently by his chair, and Walshe sat silently at his writing table. They had reached a position from which escape was not easy.

"I'm suggesting it for your convenience," said the psychiatrist, "not for any other reason. I might save you weeks of work."

"Yes, Sir," said the other, glumly non-committal. And they paused again.

"Look here, Whitfield. *Trilby's* a rattling good yarn, but it's nonsense from beginning to end. Perhaps you didn't realize that. It gives a completely false picture of what hypnosis really is. Did you know that you can't put a person to sleep without his absolute consent?"

Whitfield smiled. "It's a thing I know nothing of at all."

"All right, then. So much the better. Forget everything you've heard about it, and start from the beginning. Think of it as something normal and harmless, which it is. The fact is that we use the wrong word: we ought to say suggestion, for that is what we mean. People make suggestions to each other all day long without knowing it. I scratch my nose, and then you scratch yours: you yawn, and I follow. I only take that process a step forward. I suggest (with your consent) that you're asleep, and you fall into a doze. Then I suggest dreams to you, and you dream. The only rum thing about it is that when you dream you can remember so much more than when you're awake. That's the basis of the thing."

But Whitfield pursed his lips and shook his head: "I won't hide from you that I don't like the idea of the thing altogether. It seems wrong," he said. "Sort of unnatural."

"I see your objection," Walshe paused before saying softly and impressively: "I've got a proposition to make to you. Suppose I hypnotize someone else in front of you for a start. Suppose you see how the thing is done, you might then see for yourself that it's harmless. I think you ought to agree to my proposition, in fairness to me."

Whitfield clasped his hands and looked down at them

shyly with an absurd resemblance to a nervous girl. He was worried. He knew that unless he could get rid of his mad disposition to destroy himself, he would lose his job, and he was a married man with children. Yet even the prospect of a cure did not reconcile him to these weird rites. He felt cornered in this strange new world. But he was sensible and took the bold course.

"All right," he said at last, and sat down.

Walshe went quickly over to his house telephone and pressed one of the buttons: "Miss Kilburton? I want to show a patient effects of suggestion, so would you come along now. Thanks."

Then turning to Whitfield he said: "You'll find this rather amusing, I expect." Whitfield nodded, but with no lightening of his Northern gloom.

Miss Kilburton had often done this before for the sake of hesitant patients. She enjoyed it very much, even though it made her fall in love with Walshe who had explained long ago that he did not wish to return her passion. She was a good secretary, and an absolutely perfect subject for hypnosis, so he kept her on at a large salary even though this did involve him in occasional scenes caused by her frustrated adoration. She walked brightly into the room. "Good morning, Mr. Whitfield," she said with a gay smile full of gold-stopped teeth.

Whitfield was moved to the corner, and he watched Miss Kilburton lie on the sofa after having first modestly loosened her stays and untied her belt. "The sun's in my eyes," she said, and Walshe went over to one of the windows and drew the curtains.

"That all right?"

"Fine," said Miss Kilburton.

Walshe having got a pad and pencil from his writing-table, drew a chair to the couch and looked into her eyes.

"Relax," he said, "relax all over. Relax in your chest. Breathe deep. You're very tired. Going down, and down, and down. You're *so* sleepy. You're so sleepy, so sleepy, so sleepy, that you can't keep your eyes open. The eyelids are going down, down, down. You're *so* tired. You're sleeping deep and deep and deep."

Whitfield saw her eyelids flutter and presently she appeared to be fast asleep. Then Walshe said: "Your left hand is light. So light you can't hold it down, and it's going up, up, up." And to his amazement Whitfield saw her left arm rising till she held it perpendicularly in the air. Then he said:

"And your right hand too. It's light, light, light, and it's going up, up, up." And the same thing happened to the right arm.

Then he said: "The palms are turning inwards, they are facing each other." And this happened, too.

"And now," said Walshe, "the fingers are joining each other, and the two hands are becoming clasped together. Clasped tight! Tight! Tight!" Soon she held her hands so tightly clasped that the knuckles stood out white. "And now," went on Walshe, "your hands are coming slowly down to your chest, resting on your chest, resting gently, gently, on your chest." And the hands came down and rested on her chest, still clasped.

"And now," said Walshe, "I've got you. Haven't I?"

In a thick sleepy voice she said: "Yes."

Walshe looked over to Whitfield. "That's the first

part," he whispered. Then he turned back to Miss Kilburton: "It's this morning," he said, "and you are having breakfast in your flat at Earl's Court. And you've got a paper in your hand. A newspaper. Something's written on the newspaper. What is it?"

"On top," came the voice from another world, "it says new hair styles by Diana Wayne. Then it says Daily in squiggly writing. Then there's a picture of a lion and a horse holding a round thing and there's a crown on it. Then it says Mail in squiggly writing, and then in red Mussolini's yes or no to Paris."

"What does it say on the next line?"

"It says weather cool, and — "

"All right. What does it say below that?"

"London Manchester Paris" she chanted, and then Walshe wrote down the figures as she went on: "no one three one two four Wednesday May one eight one nine three eight one penny postage in U.K. and — "

"All right. That'll do."

He held up the pad and signalled Whitfield to take it, which he did.

"Thank you, Miss Kilburton. Now you will go fast asleep for one minute. Then you will say 'Ready.'"

She breathed deeply and Walshe turned to Whitfield once more: "There you are," he said. "It's quite simple. Nothing to be frightened of, is there?"

Whitfield stroked his jaw. "No. No there's nothing frightening. That's true. But if I was asleep there, can I be sure you might not make me say or do what I wouldn't, leastways not if I was full awake. Eh?"

"No. I told you that can't be done. I've no special

power over Miss Kilburton, though it may look as though I have. I can't make Miss Kilburton do what she doesn't want to do. I'll show you, if you like."

"How can you do that?"

"Easily. Wait till she comes to."

Soon the voice from the sofa said: "Ready."

"Miss Kilburton," said Walshe, "will you do anything I ask."

"Anything," she replied with fervour.

"Then go and jump out of the window and kill yourself," he said sharply.

Miss Kilburton gave a yawn and sat up. "Don't try to be funny with me," she said with a smile. "Oh, dear, I wish you wouldn't put me into a deep sleep in the middle of the morning. It makes me feel muzzy at lunch." She stood up wide awake. She began readjusting her stays and belt.

"Do you remember the number of today's *Daily Mail*?"

"No, of course I don't. I told it to you? Was I right?"

Walshe went over to a table at the far end of the room and got a copy of the paper. He and Whitfield compared its number with the one he had taken down.

"Quite correct," he said. "Not one mistake. Good show, my dear. All right, Miss Kilburton, that is all. Thank you very much, indeed." She left the room. He turned to Whitfield. "You see, in your mind you remember everything, even the number of a newspaper you read, though most of it is quickly buried out of reach. But by that simple method which I have shown you we can get hold of it once more. What happened to your arm is recorded there in your mind. If I can pull it out, like I pulled out that number of the *Daily Mail*, we can very likely put you straight. Are you game to have a shot?"

Whitfield licked his lips.

"All right, Sir."

"Good. We'll start tomorrow."

The room was dark because the blinds were down and the heavy curtains were drawn across the two big windows. There was only one light shining, a little reading lamp behind the couch which sent up a deep shadow so that the figure lying there was almost invisible. But the light shone on Walshe's face which was looking drawn with the effort of long concentration. He was sitting on a chair by the side of his patient.

He said: "Now you go to sleep for five minutes, and then you'll wake up, and then I'll give you a cigarette."

Whitfield fell into a deep sleep, and while he waited for him to recover consciousness Walshe drew the curtains and blinds, letting the late afternoon sun into the room. He switched out the reading lamp, and sat at his writing-table till the patient should come out of his trance. He had put him to sleep three times now, and he felt that he was approaching the solution of this odd case. Before him, on his table, he had the relevant documents spread out neatly so that he could see them all at a glance. There were X-ray photographs of the arm with a report from a bone specialist, reports from the doctors he had

seen at Sheffield and Harrogate, a detailed report of his
engineering experience by Berrington, a brief description of his childhood dictated by himself to Miss Kilburton, and a record of his war service. Walshe picked out
the latter, and when five minutes were up he said gently:
"Are you waking up, Whitfield?"

There was a heavy yawn from the sofa. Slowly and
clumsily Whitfield sat up, lowered his feet to the floor,
stared about him, and shook his head. He cleared his
throat and yawned again. "All right," he said in a sleepy
voice, "I'm waking up." He stretched out a hand as
though looking for something. Walshe said: "Your collar and tie are just by you on the chair there."

Whitfield stood up and dressed himself. He had taken
off his coat and waistcoat, collar and tie. When he was
fully dressed again Walshe pointed to the armchair by
his writing-table and said: "Now come over here and I'll
discuss with you what I've found out. I really believe
we are getting to the bottom of your case. Come along."

Whitfield walked over to the chair, but just as he was
about to sit down he grabbed hold of Walshe's arm.

"Give me a cigarette," he said in a sharp anxious tone.

"The cigarettes are over there at the far end of the
room. Help yourself."

But Whitfield still held his arm. "You give one to me,"
he cried.

"All right."

Walshe led him over to the table at the far end where
the cigarette box and matches were standing on a tray.
He offered him the open box. Whitfield grabbed a cigarette and lit it. Then he stopped, looking embarrassed.

"Excuse me, Sir," he said, "excuse me. I — I beg your pardon."

Walshe laughed. "Don't do that. When you were asleep I told you I'd give you a cigarette, and now you're seeing to it that I do. You are a very good subject. It's because your mind is firm, orderly, direct; no nonsense about you. We'll soon get to the bottom of your trouble."

They went back to the writing-table and Walshe explained the case to Whitfield.

"Our next job," he said, "is to concentrate on your war service because that is where this arm business began. I'm sure of that. We've delved pretty deep in your memory and you've taken me over several periods of your past life. I've seen you as a foreman and engineer in Mr. Berrington's works, and as a soldier in the West Yorkshire regiment, and as a kid at school, and as a small child; and wherever I've been with you in this journey round your memory I've asked how you felt about your arm, and you've told me. You have confidence in me. But although you've told me how you feel, you've never told me *why* you feel as you do. When you're an engineer, in fact any time after 1920, you tell me you hate your arm. You call it 'my bloody arm,' and you hang on to that word 'bloody.' You say you want to get rid of it. You say it's a bad wicked bloody arm, and that it doesn't belong to you. 'Send the bloody thing away' you cry out. Always that word 'bloody.' Tell me, are you a man who swears a good deal?"

Whitfield, looking exactly like a Methodist chapel, shook his head.

"That's what I thought." Walshe peered at Whitfield's war record, "You were demobbed in 1920. That's the date, isn't it?"

"Correct."

"That's the dividing line. Any time after 1920 it's your 'bloody arm,' but before then it's something you're shy of, though without anger. You don't use the word 'bloody,' for example.

"As we go farther back into the war you get vague about it, until we lose it altogether sometime in the summer of '17. Before then you've nothing to tell me. I believe we can narrow it down to that summer. Something happened then. What do you say?"

Whitfield shook his head: "I remember nothing, Sir."

Walshe passed a hand over his face. He sighed.

"Can you tell me what this is about: 'Mentioned in despatches 23rd of June 1917.' What happened then?"

"I was in a forward patrol. We had to clear some detached enemy trenches which looked as if they'd been abandoned in a big straightening of Jerry's line, and we wanted them so as to straighten our line."

"This is interesting. Tell me more about it."

"It was early morning, only half light and our patrol had to move into these trenches. You was expecting to see a Jerry round every corner, and from what happened, it did look, afterwards like, as if we'd been spotted as we came over No Man's Land."

"Did you find any Jerries?"

"No. There wasn't any. They'd all cleared out."

"Why do you think you'd been spotted?"

"While we was in, Jerry lobs over a shell right on to

these here trenches, and I'm buried in earth. Knocked
right out I was, and I'd have been suffocated if our sergeant-major hadn't spotted me."

"Was your arm not hurt?"

"No, Sir."

"How long were you knocked out for?"

"Ooh! Fair matter of fifteen minutes."

Walshe thought in silence before speaking. "It's just
possible that something happened to do with your arm
on that patrol."

As he was being driven in his smart Bentley from
Hampstead to Harley Street, on Thursday morning,
Walshe went over the case in his mind. Here in Whitfield there was, as far as he could see, one single maladjustment, and only one, and this, and nothing else, made
him dangerously eccentric. If the case was really as beautifully simple as it seemed, success, total and neat, was
for once within his grasp.

He arrived at the house in Harley Street, and having
put away his hat and coat, he walked straight up to his
consulting-room on the second floor. He saw with pleasure that his writing-table was bare except for a single
dossier. He had given instructions to Miss Kilburton that
on this morning he wished to have no other appointments, as he foresaw that hard work would be required
to reach down into that depth where Whitfield's obses-
sion lay embedded. He pressed a button on his house-
telephone.

"Miss Kilburton? To tell you I am here. Show Whitfield up as soon as he arrives."

"He's coming in now."

"Good."

He went over to where the newspapers lay like fishes in a row, picked up *The Times*, and rolled it longwise so that it resembled a paper stick.

"Hallo, Whitfield," he said as his patient was shown in. "Let's get down to work straight away."

"All right, Sir."

"Your arm. Are you feeling the pain?"

Whitfield shook his head and pursed his lips. "It's there, you know. I'm sorry but I can't say as there's any improvement."

"Oh, but there shouldn't be." Walshe smiled with smug triumph. He added: "When we find the answer I expect the pain to vanish instantly."

While Whitfield took off his coat and waistcoat, collar and tie, Walshe switched on the reading lamp and drew the blinds and curtains. The room was once more dark.

Whitfield lay on the couch, Walshe sat on the chair and began once more the act of hypnosis.

In a little more than five minutes Whitfield became a young lance-corporal once more, speaking with a slightly more plebeian accent than his usual one, using a few obscene army expressions but not so many as most soldiers do. He was in the frontline trenches, feeling constant fear. He and Walshe together, one for the first time, the other for the second time, reached the sector of the line where young Whitfield had been stationed on the 23rd of June of the year 1917, but as he recognized the time and the place Whitfield suddenly woke up. " 'Ere, wher' am I?" he cried.

"All right," said Walshe, "you're here. I went a little too fast for you. Don't worry. Just relax. Relax your limbs, relax this arm here . . ." in less than a minute Whitfield was in a trance once more, and Walshe took him by very slow stages back into his life until they reached his days in the army once more, and then by gradual steps he led him gently and reassuringly, much more slowly than before, back to the 23rd of June of 1917 . . .

" 'Ere you, Nobby," gasped Whitfield, "where's me rifle?" Walshe put the rolled up copy of *The Times* into his right hand . . .

Once more Whitfield was crawling behind Nobby in the French mud. He felt the morning breeze on his cheek, and he followed, slowly, alert, and inwardly stupid with fear. He could hear the distant rumble of the guns in the silence of the front line. He crawled slowly and expertly over Walshe's carpet.

He looked back to see if the man behind, Hicks, was still there. He kept a short way behind Nobby. They reached the trenches which were of moderate depth. They lowered themselves one after another. Whitfield looked old and pale. The trenches were empty. No one in the dug-outs. So they felt a little better but they knew they had not seen everything yet. The officer was signing and Whitfield and Nobby and young Hicks went to him. He whispered orders to them. "Whitfield, you'll go down that way. Listen. These trenches don't look to connect back. Want to make sure — otherwise no use to us. They look to go sixty yards down that way, then stop. Have a look. Careful of booby-traps. I'm going this way.

Clarke and Hicks come with me. Sergeant-Major you stay here till we're back." Then Whitfield went by himself, gritting his teeth, down the trenches, very slowly. He had to walk sixty yards and then back. His imagination was kept down by the weight of the heavy stupidity of fear. So he crept down the trench, down what seemed that great distance, peering into and then swiftly entering and leaving a dug-out, making sure, not daring to hope, until he saw that he was nearing the end before which there was a corner. As silently as he could, making hardly any sound on the duck-boards and dry mud, he came at last to the corner. And then, when he rounded it, he saw, towering over him, a man. Once again he looked and made out clearly the awful shape of that which had cursed his life from then on, no matter how long he might live.

Walshe was watching intently as he stole down the wall. Then what happened, happened so quickly that a less agile observer might have completely missed its significance. Whitfield staggered back half a pace, and with the effort of raising a heavy rifle swung the rolled-up *Times* above his shoulder, and in a voice choked in his throat by terror he cried: "Tike yer hands down!" and swung the paper forward and down with all his great strength, hitting a light-bracket. The lampshade was flung into the corner and the bulb shattered. All this happened in a flash. The noise of the bursting bulb did not awake him from his trance. Walshe saw that in the act of striking he had leaned forward in such a way that his left hand had slipped away from the roll of paper. He was left holding this roll, with the effort of a man holding a rifle by the top of the barrel, in his right hand. He said: "Coo." Then suddenly, with a wild leap, he dropped the roll, flung up his hands for protection to his head, and fell unconscious to the ground, forwards and with crossed legs, exactly as he had done more than twenty years ago in France. . . .

Half an hour later Whitfield was sitting in the armchair by Walshe's writing-table.

"It all happened," said Walshe, "just as we thought, on the 23rd of June in 1917. That shell-burst not only removed the memory of the fifteen minutes which followed, but of a minute or so which preceded it. Contrary to what your people believed there really was a German in those trenches. He was hiding from you behind the last corner of the trench. You remember going down a trench alone?"

He nodded.

"Well, there he was, and you came on him. He probably tried to surrender but you weren't taking any chances with him, and you hit out at him with the butt end of your rifle. You finished the blow holding the rifle with your right hand. That's very important. You certainly knocked him out, and you seemed at the time to have killed him — probably did. You used all your strength. But before you'd time to make sure — bang, down comes this shell and buries you both. That's the end of him. That's the end of what happened.

"Now, you'd been brought up to believe that to kill is wicked. This act of yours, got hidden straightaway, owing to concussion, in your subconscious mind. In your military life, when killing was the order of the day, you like every one else had to unlearn and readjust a lot of your behaviour patterns. But in your subconscious you had a sense of guilt. When you left the army, then that hidden sense of guilt became prominent. We are all raving mad below conscious life, but we are logical just the same. Your hatred of your arm — your bloody arm — increased till it expressed itself in your higher mind by a sense of pain, and every now and again in climaxes, which we have not yet been able to analyse, and may not have to. It is clear though that in these climaxes you tried to destroy the limb which had committed this atrocity. By smashing up your arm you were trying to be finally dissociated from the sin it had committed for you.

"Do you follow me quite clearly?"

Whitfield had changed in appearance. His usual look of smug calm had vanished. He was breathing silently but deeply through his open mouth. He was white in the face, sweat was running down his forehead on to his nose and neck, and there was a look of extreme fear in the expression of his eyes.

"No, you've not made it clear, Sir. I don't follow at all. Have I just dreamt about this German in these trenches, or did this really happen? I don't understand that."

Walshe looked at him, surprised at the degree of horror the explanation had produced on his patient. He hoped there was not going to be some last minute complication in this wonderfully clear case. The unintelligence of Whitfield's question disquieted him.

"Now keep calm, man," he said. "Have a cigarette.

Our long sessions seem to have rather knocked you up. Would you prefer to postpone discussion till this evening? I'm free then. Cigarette."

He pushed the cigarette box towards him. Whitfield took no notice of this invitation. Clasping his hands, and with heavily asserted self-control, he said:

"I'd like to hear about it right now. Everything. Did I only dream all this under hypnotism, or did it really happen sometime else?"

"It happened on that 23rd of June."

Whitfield was leaning forward, trying to take this in. He gave a little inward gasp. "I killed a man?"

"Well . . . perhaps. You tried to and perhaps succeeded."

He began drumming the fingers of his clasped hands. "And if I didn't, what then?"

"I don't know," Walshe replied with a smile. "Was there no talk of a German having been found in those trenches?"

This remark irritated Whitfield.

"No," he said. "No, there wasn't. None. None at all. I'd remember if there was." He calmed down. "Don't you think," he went on, "don't you think that if I didn't kill him, then he must have suffocated in that huge mass of earth which came over us?"

"I couldn't answer that without seeing the ground."

"Well, I can answer. Either I killed him outright as the poor devil tried to surrender, or I left him to suffocate in that heap of muck. What a thing to do."

"You had no conscious memory of him when you came to."

"That's not the point. *It's what I did*."

The tragic intensity of Whitfield's last words drew Walshe up sharply and he was silent in perplexity. Because he had grown used to the direct good sense of this patient he had laid aside the tedious subtlety he required for the handling of his more usual ones, but he saw now that he must exercise all his gifts of tact and cunning. And then, as he was about to say something suitable, Whitfield suddenly broke into a paroxysm of weeping.

Walshe came quickly to the arm-chair and stood over him. "Come now, pull yourself together," he said in a sharp voice. "This all happened years ago."

Whitfield cried out, gasped rather through his dry tearless sobs: "But it happened. That's the point. It happened and I did it. I can hardly believe . . . and it's true."

Walshe pulled his chair forward and sat opposite Whitfield. "I can well understand that what I have told you has come as a frightful shock. To have anything so big as a death stowed away in your subconscious is painful in itself, and its release into your waking mind must be very painful too. But try to look at it in this way: you have now been set free. The reason of the pain in your arm, your efforts to destroy your arm and yourself, were because you could never understand, down in that chaos, that there was no guilt attaching to this particular deed. You were a soldier. It was your duty. But in your subconscious you knew nothing of soldiers or duty. You were horribly caught there in an utterly unescapable feeling that you had done wrong. And now at last you *have* escaped. There is no guilt. I take it you're not a conscientious objector?"

Whitfield shook his head.

"Well then — and, even if you were, you had no possible sort of blame in this thing. What you did was quite evidently done in self-defence."

"You said he tried to surrender."

Walshe made a sound of impatience.

"He put up a hand and you said 'Take it down.' Quite likely he raised his hand to strike you."

On hearing, from one who had heard it, the actual words he had used, Whitfield was again overwhelmed by emotion. He covered his face, and there came from him once more the hideous dry sobs which seemed to rend his whole frame. He tried to master himself, put down his hands and looked up at Walshe, a repulsively ugly picture of degradation and a sense of sin. "And I have a wife," he groaned, "and children."

As Walshe told me the story when we were together in Africa, he paused here. He told it with much skill and I felt that at this moment, when Whitfield broke down, he paused so that I could imagine, without his marring the performance by repetitions, that Whitfield protested his guilt, and Walshe his innocence, for a long time, without either influencing the other.

"There was nothing to be done," Walshe said to me, "nothing at all. He was so appalled by the discovery of his murder that no rational argument could alter his mind. I had monkeyed about with his subconscious with the result that I had carefully lifted a murder from beyond the reaches of his senses into the very midst of his life. And I had thereby transformed him from a first-class engineer with a pain in his arm and an infrequent tendency to blackouts, into an utterly broken despairing semi-lunatic, a plague to himself and to every one he knew."

"What about his arm?" I said.

"That came out just as I expected. Before he left me —and I thought this might clinch matters in my favour — I asked him how his arm felt. 'Funny thing,' he said, 'the pain's gone. Quite gone.'

" 'Well,' I said, 'don't you see why?'

"He gazed at me. 'I do,' he said.

" 'And don't you see,' I went on, feeling a cheap chattering little bounder in front of that image of human guilt, 'that that means no more blackouts, means you've no more cause to worry about your job, means I can ring up Mr. Berrington at this moment and say: "You need have no fears about Whitfield, you can promote him as high as you like. He's now a perfectly balanced reliable man."?'

" 'It means,' said Whitfield, 'that I am a man who killed another man. It means, like it says in the Bible, that I bear the mark of Cain.'

"It was me against the Bible."

"He left me. I had done all I could. There was nothing else for me to do."

"But what in fact did you do?" I asked.

"I rang up Berrington in Sheffield. I told him that Whitfield's arm was now set right, and I explained briefly what had been the cause of the pain and the mysterious fainting fits. I told him that treatment had badly shaken his nerves, as it often does, and I recommended that he should be given a holiday. Berrington was a nice fellow — quite a Cheeryble in his way. He told me he'd give Whitfield a week with his family at Scarborough. I said I would like to see Whitfield at the end of his holiday if he could be sent to London for a day. He agreed."

"So you saw Whitfield again?"

Walshe smiled as the scene of his last meeting with his patient came back to him.

"When he came into my consulting-room after his holiday I believed for a moment that after all I had made a cure, that I wasn't such a dud as I had supposed. Whitfield was tanned by the sun, we had a wonderful Spring that year, and he walked in with the self-confident, determined look which I remembered. He looked healthy and happy, and as he held out his big right hand he smiled with a sort of mischievous jollity, as I'd never seen him do before."

" 'Well,' I said, 'I needn't ask how you are. You look fine. I'm afraid I worked you very hard and shook you up. But you're all right now, aren't you?'

" 'Yes, I am,' he said, 'I'm as fit as a fiddle. And I want to ask you to forgive me for breaking down like that last time I was here. You must have thought me an awful weakling. I'm sorry. I apologize, Sir.'

" 'My dear man, don't think you need do that. I was only worried at the time that the shock of discovery might prove too much for you. It was certainly enough to give the hardiest a nasty jolt.'

" 'Oh you mean about me and coshing a German?'

" 'Yes.'

"Whitfield smiled with some embarrassment. 'I'm afraid I got very hysterical when I was here before — started imagining a lot of things. Killing Germans! It was the effect on me of this hypnosis of yours, that's all. Forget it please.'

" 'I don't quite follow. You have got used to the idea now, haven't you?'

"Whitfield laughed. 'For mercy's sake, Sir. Who d'you think I am? Can you see me killing another man?'

" 'You were a soldier.'

" 'Yes, I was. And I suppose you might say that that sort of thing might easily have come my way. Thankful it never did, that's what I am. It's a terrible thing to kill another man. Particularly hand to hand. Terrible!'

" 'But on that day in June — '

" 'No, Sir. If I killed a German I'd know it all right. It was all imagination, just childish fancy, what I told you. It never took place. Never.'

" 'Whitfield, you'd be much happier in the end if you faced the facts. What happened — '

"But he looked me full in the face, and although he was a friendly sort of man, I saw in him a look, a faint look, of defiant fanatical anger. 'I know what happened,' he said, 'I was there, not you. You acted for the best, but this hypnotism of yours, it isn't really made for people like me. I suppose it's because I'm not educated like I'd ought to be. No, Sir, you must not take what I said when you put me to sleep all that serious. It was childish fancy. Nothing more nor less. Just childish fancy.'

"I saw then that he was a hopeless case.

" 'Tell me,' I said, 'how's your arm?'

" 'Not too bad, thank you. It's always this way. After treatment it's as right as pie, then the trouble comes back again. I can feel it these last two days. It's there, not so as to hurt me good and proper, but it's there.'

" 'Whitfield,' I said, 'I can only tell you this. You must keep away from machines at work. Don't go near them. They encourage your blackouts.'

" 'Thank you for that advice,' he answered, impressed at last by something I said. 'I'll be careful to bear that in mind.' "

A negro servant came out from the hotel ringing a little gong to tell us that dinner was ready. When we had finished our drinks, Walshe and I walked slowly towards the dining verandah. For a little we said nothing and then I asked him what he thought about the case now. "There was something in that man's remark about education," answered Walshe, after a pause. "We say that uneducated people are credulous, but often they suffer from the opposite fault: a profound innate scepticism . . . deep down he could *not* believe . . ." This was a new idea to me, and I found it impressive. We stopped before going into the verandah, and Walshe went on: "A person of more compelling personality than myself might have succeeded in curing him; that is another possible explanation of my wretched failure. But since this morning I incline to a yet more humbling one: what I needed was more expert knowledge of my art, knowledge such as that wonderful witch-doctor must have over there." And he nodded gravely towards the river, which was flashing in the light of the rising moon, and towards the great dark forests on the shore.

"Perhaps bad education has made me too sceptical," I answered, "but I don't believe in noble savages."

☼ *The Interview*

In our miserable day it has become fashionable for people to dwell on the woes which attend abundant fortune. To insist on the ugly side of success; on its vulgarity and its absurdity; on the discoloured and uncomely breast which plenty offers to her few favoured children, has become an exquisite refinement of an age condemned to envy. All the same, not many people would renounce success on account of its reward. Louis Gisborough, a rich man whose fame extended to at least a million of his fellow-beings, was not entirely unhappy.

He was a distinguished writer who was also extremely popular; his books sold in hundreds of thousands; he was rich for that honourable reason. He lived in a pretty, pleasantly furnished house situated in the forest of Chantilly and surrounded by a well-ordered garden through which ran a trout stream. Being endowed with common sense he understood precisely the extent of his extreme good luck, and, as must presently appear, his nature was ill-adapted to grief. If, in conformity with fashion, he knew the pain of constant regret, he knew it most often and sincerely as a sense of irritation that although he had so much to rejoice in, he could rejoice so little. He was in a sense unhappy that he was incapable of a state of constant joy; that he was impotent, in a manner of speaking.

He had been famous for over forty years, and he had lived in France since the end of the First Great War. He liked living in a foreign country where he was not forced into intimacy with a great number of people whom he did not know (a freak of circumstance which comes with literary success); but yet, when gradually his fame followed him to Paris and his peace was slowly disturbed, he was not altogether displeased. The French have traditions widely different from the English which make them treat writers as people of profound consequence, and a writer needs to be peculiarly free of vanity not to enjoy this. Louis Gisborough enjoyed it very much.

His excursions from Chantilly were infrequent, but for all this he had become quite a recognized figure of Paris. Visitors from England used to note him at receptions in the British Embassy, where he was always careful to make regular appearances. On first meetings his admirers could not help feeling disappointed. He did not look at all like a literary man, let alone a distinguished one. His face had the expressionless plainness of a potato; his hanging sandy moustache obliterated any sign of sensitiveness which might have been visible in the mouth; his eyes, in spite of an uninterrupted look of surprise given to them by highly placed eyebrows, showed no sign of curiosity or of deep feeling. What you saw, as you looked at Louis Gisborough, was an obese and somewhat elderly English gentleman, usually wearing a neat dark suit of old-fashioned and ample cut, a starched open collar with a bow tie, and, when out of doors, a soft grey trilby with edges turned down, which seemed to be half a size too big for him. That hat, alone, carried certain Bohemian suggestions with it, except that it might as easily have been the hat of a broad-minded diplomat or of an eccentric sportsman, as the hat of a master of English prose.

In conversation this famous writer tended to avoid literary subjects. When, as often happened, he was forced to discuss such things, a faint note of bitterness was sometimes audible, and a perspicacious listener might have discovered from this that one cause of his success was that he aimed much farther and higher than the target he struck.

For instance, one evening in 1948, a lady said to him in Paris: "And what do you think about this book they make such praise about, *The Heart of the Matter*, which is from Grryeam Grreene?"

"A very remarkable performance. I like the delineation of figure and the construction. I cannot say more as it's all about the soul, and for me the soul is simply a word I use when I need to sound a deep note. I might as well say Boom for all I know about it. Religious people tell me that I too have a soul, and I find that a most flattering proposition, indeed I should love to believe that there was the slightest reason to suppose it true. You must read Graham Greene to discover why it might be. You should read me for conversation, perfect grammar, descriptions of attractive houses, and unfortunate love affairs. That sort of stuff. Do you like my books?"

"But of course I do like them."

"Then I shouldn't read Mr. Greene's books if I were you. They go in for all the sort of things mine don't. People commit sins in his books, and regret it deeply. They pray in churches. Now if a person in one of my books goes to church he is moved by the sight of an innocent young girl to remember a passion which once consumed him, and is now burnt to ashes. I am superficial."

He spoke, with hardly a change of expression, in a soft pedantic voice, and it was natural to assume that his self-disparagement was a kind of banter. So far as he knew no one had guessed that he spoke at such times with complete sincerity.

In common with most men he enjoyed melodrama, and when he spoke thus he was giving himself vulgar delight by unguarding the secret he carried about with him, and which he was prepared to defend with his life.

As part of his professional duties he often went back to memories of youthful experience in order to reconstruct scenes for his novels with precision, and to examine the emotions with which they were connected. At such times he had more than once seemed to himself like a man walking down the neat ranks of a morgue, prompted by some assiduous and decent-spoken official to identify corpses. Nothing which had happened to him meant much to him now. Long ago he had put all the feeling which was within him into literary shape, in the fashion of a bronze-worker pouring bright hot liquid into a mould. Unknown to his admirers he had run out of metal midway in his career, since when he had produced imitations made of cleverly tinted plaster. He knew that his skill was not enough to disguise his deceit for ever, but he hoped that the moment of discovery would occur after his lifetime. While he was in the flesh he preferred that no one should know that he was among the dead.

Catherine Gisborough, the daughter of this eminent novelist, was a pretty girl of twenty-three. She bore a resemblance to Gisborough in the distant way a handsome young woman can do to a very plain elderly father; she had similar features without the potato effect, and adorned by the brighter, more vivid, colouring of her mother. As the child of divorced parents she had lived since she remembered in a state of unwilling independence, until in the war she had gladly renounced this for the stabler pattern of a life of State service, and to this she clung. After the war she remained a clerk in the Foreign Office, finding in that dark cold place the parental guardianship she had missed. She remained there until she became engaged to be married to a young man called Robert Ferrers. He was precisely what husbands and sons-in-laws are expected to be; five years older than his girl, and doing remarkably well as a beginner at the bar. He was so very self-assured that his nervousness at the prospect of meeting his father-in-law, Louis Gisborough, surprised Catherine a good deal. When he came to her flat to take her to dinner one evening she said:

"After tackling my mother so boldly, what on earth frightens you about Papa?"

"Oh, I liked your mother. She's easy to get on with."

Catherine said: "Oh, yes, she's easy to get on with,"

and looked depressed, without his seeing. Before she had time to say more Ferrers went on:

"A father minds losing his daughter more than a mother does, the same as a mother minds losing a son. It's inevitable, a sort of rhythm in Nature I'd call it. I don't mind hiding from you that I'm pretty terrified at the prospect of meeting your father."

"Papa's an old poppet."

"To you, I dare say, not to me. Why the dickens should he be? As far as he's concerned I'm merely the man who's going to take away the prop of his declining years — like a practical joke; like pulling away your chair as you sit down."

"But look at the telegram he sent us." Gisborough had conveyed his approval in simple and moving terms, adding a request that Ferrers should come and visit him at Chantilly, an excursion for which he asked that he might pay all expenses.

"I dare say he's very kind," said Ferrers, "but for all that he must really dislike me like poison. It's not a question of individual character, it's a question of human nature plain and simple. Affectionate fathers don't like the men who cart off their daughters, unless the carters-off are so rich and powerful that they can smother the pain with gold and glory."

"Well, you're going to be very rich, and you're quite respectable."

"Hm . . . 'Going to be' . . . and only 'quite respectable.' You don't understand this problem at all. Glory! That's what's needed."

"You got the M.C."

"But I need the Garter just now. It's no use kidding yourself — that man's not going to like me, and I'm windy."

They embraced with desperate mutual desire. They were sitting in the main room of her flat which was in a big apartment-block in Westminster, a room which had begun to show those signs of giving up appearances which come over a place soon to be left by tenants. A curtain drooped clumsily from a defective rail, because the expense of mending it was not now worth while. In every part of the room there was some such sign of forgotten affection.

"My father is a curious man" she said, in the calm inappropriate voice women can use suddenly on amorous occasions, unconcerned that this ordinary remark had been preceded by a near-equivalent of the carnal act of love and its dark mysteries. "You'll probably find him a funny old stick, rather garrulous and very much interested in our house arrangements, and servant problems, and that sort of thing. Not in the least my idea of a great literary genius. You'll be able to talk to him about fishing, too. He once caught a sixty-pound salmon in Norway."

"You promise he won't talk about his books."

"Oh, no. He never talks about his books." And she added with a laugh: "Only to very pretty women who can't understand."

"Or literature?"

"No. Only to girls. He's rather like I imagine a scientist to be. If you met Einstein he wouldn't expect you to discuss relativity with him."

"All the same . . . if I was going to marry Einstein's daughter, he might be a bit put out if he found out that I thought the earth was flat. You've no idea how ill-read I am. I've never read anything at all except what I've had to. I've read nothing by Shakespeare except *Richard II* and *Hamlet*, and that was because I was forced to at school. Nothing by Dickens. Nothing by Thackeray. Nothing by Milton, and I don't believe I know the names of any others. As far as I'm concerned the great authors of the world just wasted their time."

She smiled at him and said she loved him for being so honest.

The Summer had been so hot in France that one looked forward to the cool of Autumn as one does in more southerly climates. Mr. Gisborough was sitting under a plane tree. He laid the book he was reading by his side on the bench, and looked at the scene about him. His garden consisted of a long lawn which extended for fifty yards from the house, and was surrounded by trees. Beyond the lawn, on the far side of a row of young birches, lay a group of formal beds, and to the right of them, from the house, a half-acre of kitchen garden. On one side the forest came up to the very wall of his property, and he looked at the mass of leaves in the sunlight, shining no longer with the liquid glitter of Spring, but with a hard glare which showed, amid abundance of green, a few dead colours. There were no clouds in the sky, and the day was still, yet occasional slight breezes felt cooler than those of a month ago, and told of a merciful decline of the excessive heat which the creatures on this earth had had to live through, as the sun moved away from the Summer tropic.

With his book Mr. Gisborough had brought with him the letter which he had received a month ago from his daughter telling him of her engagement to Robert Ferrers, and with which she had sent some photographs. The envelope lay in the book, marking his place. He now drew it out, and looked at the pictures of the young man who was coming to lunch with him that day. Luncheon, as he carefully called it.

Ferrers was evidently handsome in the muscular athletic style. According to Catherine he had played cricket for his school, for his college at the University, and once for his county. Following the convention of his time Louis Gisborough had tended in his works to describe athletes as figures of absurdity, and he smiled to himself as he admitted that a "clean-limbed" cricketer gave him an irresistible sense of assurance. He was distinctly pleased about this element of cricket, though he was a little humiliated at finding himself reacting to the problem with such crude Englishry.

He loved his daughter; that was understood. In so far as a man who only felt strongly about grammar, and could not eat without debating inwardly the correct use of repasts in fiction; in so far as such a man could love, he loved his daughter. He had inducements to do so: she had an open, honest character, was very pretty, and had never given him the smallest trouble. She was obviously nice. With no morbid intention, merely to examine the state of his mind, as he might examine his typewriter, he would sometimes picture to himself what would be his feelings if he were to receive terrible news about Catherine: that she was dead, for example. There was no doubt that he would be acutely distressed, and that he would be moved to tears. After that his imagination could not take him further, and he had to rely on mathematical calculations. He had had a mistress once who died of peritonitis in 1928. As a result of this calamity he had felt cut off from the world by sorrow for as much as three months, and the wound had caused him pain for nearly a year. Allowing for a further drying up of his heart since that episode, he felt safe in estimating the effects in time of his daughter's death at five months at least. He could not help being a little shocked at the result. He treasured up his affection for Catherine as a once rich man will turn miser. He was agreeably conscious of some sorrow as he reflected that after her marriage she would no longer come alone to him to spend part of her holidays.

"Yes, Mademoiselle?" he asked as his housekeeper sailed up to him from across the lawn.

"The guest of Monsieur?" she asked of him in return. "He will remain for two nights, or three? I would wish to know, as if the gentleman is staying longer than two nights I must have changes of linen ready. Can Monsieur tell me definitively?"

She was a corpulent lady from Lorraine whose hot black clothing kept her in a state of constant sweating. She made his house clean and orderly, and yet seemed incapable of introducing any great degree of these refinements into her own person. The mention of matters even distantly related to sex caused her to blush and smile strangely. He guessed that she believed sexual intercourse to involve more violence than is usual in fact.

"Do you know who my guest is?"

"No, Monsieur."

He said, speaking more slowly than his slow custom:

"He is the young man who is engaged to be married to my daughter. She has accepted to marry him but I have never met him."

Her two red hands rushed to her cheeks and she opened her mouth like a fish's as she cried, "Oh!"

Any of her own countrymen would have been overwhelmed by rage in these circumstances, and she found it hard to believe that this Englishman was really as unconcerned as he appeared. He went on:

"So you see, Mademoiselle, we must do all in our power to make him happy and welcome. That is why I wish the best bedroom to be ready for him. It is doubtful whether he will stay the night, he probably will not, in fact, but if he does I want him to have the bedroom he will have when he comes here with his bride. That is the right thing, as you will agree. He will only be staying one night, if as much, so you need not bother about the linen."

"I did not know of this great happiness in Monsieur's family," said Mademoiselle, swaying to and fro, and blushing so dark a colour that he wondered whether this gross-minded creature had fancied some double meaning in his remarks.

"Thank you for those kind words, Mademoiselle . . . The young man should arrive between half-past twelve and one. Tell Henri that I will meet him here in the

garden. We shall eat at half-past one. Ten minutes before luncheon, let Henri bring us some sherry wine here.
At luncheon we will drink Montrachet. We will have
our coffee and liqueurs out here once more. Is that all
clear?"

"Perfectly, Monsieur."

Ferrers was in that uncomfortable and by no means
uncommon state when vitality is lowered by every
chance circumstance. He found his command of the
French language less than he had expected. He felt
younger than usual, as though he had mysteriously dis-
carded more years than he could afford. He felt weak,
clumsy, and timid; and as though he were bound for
some long and terrible exile he thought of the green fields
and old parish churches of his native country. The train
went slowly on its way from the Gare du Nord to Chantilly. He sat in a full second-class carriage. He sometimes
looked out of the window at the landscape, and sometimes grasped and then let go of a large brown-coloured
book which he had bought in London before starting
on this journey. Once or twice he opened this book and
read a few words before shutting it. It seemed to him
useless to start reading a book of seven hundred pages
while on a journey lasting less than forty-five minutes.
In the wanderings of an anxious mind he speculated for
a while on how fast it was possible to read, and whether
contests had ever been arranged in order to establish
such records of speed. He noticed that the man sitting
opposite to him, and who was wearing gloves despite the
heat of the day, was looking at him through pince-nez

glasses, as though in some anger. He wondered why this unknown man should dislike him, not having noticed the disagreeable noise he made as he shuffled his feet ceaselessly on the floor of the carriage.

An hour later he felt his weak spirits weakening a little more at the sight of Gisborough's hall, with its solemn cold stone beauty of the late eighteenth century, and its pair of marble-topped tables placed by the wall for the reception of hats and coats. In the presence of so much rich and discreet elegance he felt younger and clumsier than he had done hitherto, even on that day of youth and blunder.

From his post under the large umbrageous plane tree Mr. Gisborough saw the white coat of the servant flash into the sun, followed by the tall powerful frame of Ferrers. At the latter he looked carefully. The young man was frowning, and this gave to his face a handsome but somewhat unpleasant expression such as is depicted in busts of the Emperor Lucius Verus, or of the superb and horrible Caracalla. He noticed that as he followed Henri across the lawn Ferrers walked crookedly, and that this gait contrasted strangely with the severe eyes under their frowning Roman brows. At last, as the young man came near, Gisborough saw that uncertainty was expressed not only by the walk but in his face too. The eyes glared imperiously, but uneasily.

When two people unknown to each other are due to meet on an important occasion they are foolish if they do not prepare speeches beforehand. Gisborough had taken this precaution. Ferrers, in the train, had tried to, but without success, because his thoughts had been distracted by a mocking day dream in which, by some strange means, he first met Gisborough in a court of law. His preparations had not gone beyond a vague resolve, as he could think of nothing better, to be forthright and simple, and clear, a determination which accounted for the frown which deepened a little as the two men met in the shade. The servant bowed and vanished. They shook hands. Their eyes met horribly. And then Gisborough, anxious to avoid any silences, asked him some conventional questions. The young man stammered as he told about his journey that morning, and about his hotel in Paris. He was disturbed by the majestic quiet of the place. To a further inquiry he said "What," and regretted that word, when he realized that it had been spoken in answer to an invitation to sit down.

"Let me offer you a cigarette," said Gisborough, as they sat down together.

"Thank you very much." He took one and lit it, and leaned back on the bench, awkwardly and self-consciously, so as to avoid sitting forwards, alert, as in caricatures of such occasions.

Bearing no trace now of his frown, he looked about him with a mad smile.

Speaking in his very softest voice, Gisborough went back to the subject of travel.

"You arrived from London last night, did you?"

"Yes."

"By the Golden Arrow, I suppose?"

"No, I flew here. You save yourself a lot of bother at the customs that way." In the summery peace of the garden Ferrers seemed to be crushed by vast and terrible pressures. He knew that if he had mistaken his feelings for Catherine, he would know now, in this drowning agony.

"You prefer to fly, do you?" Gisborough went on. "Now I prefer the long journey. It makes me feel I am going a long way, as indeed one is, when one leaves England for France. I believe I would even rather enjoy the customs, if I were a little younger."

"The customs? You *enjoy* them?"

Ferrers intended these words to sound worldly-wise, but in his pain he could only speak them in an earnest and distressed manner, as though he wished to help.

"Oh, well, not exactly enjoy perhaps," replied Gisborough, unable to hide some irritation.

He found the young man's shyness catching. There was an uncomfortably long pause, an unavoidable one, during which, while Ferrers continued in deathly silence by his side, Gisborough found himself visiting that part of his mental furniture where he had collected some psychological knowledge. He had read much about the animosity of the old to the oncoming generation. He had a swift dim vision of Neanderthal fathers crunching the bones of children, of an aged figure in skins horribly transfixing a youth amid the wails of the tribe; he saw ritual castrations.

Gisborough broke the silence.

"Well," he said with an agreeable smile, "you came to talk to me about something else."

Ferrers had altered since Gisborough last spoke to him. Having struck the bottom of the sea, he was now rising at immense speed. He was a vigorous young man, not shy in ordinary circumstances, used to success; and he now set himself to dash through to the attainment of his objective, which was Gisborough's approval, with no too over-cautious regard for consequences, so that if he should create some needless havoc on the wayside — well, as he said to himself, that was just too bad! He had never failed in anything he had tried so far. What he needed here, he recognized, as he quickly surveyed his weapons and forces, or took a last view of his brief before entering court (for he still hankered for the paraphernalia of the law), was a strong bold display of honesty, as sincere as possible under the circumstances.

He looked at his cigarette for a moment while his mouth, as Gisborough noticed, became depressed in a truly hideous grimace of determination. In the repulsive fashion of the army he spat out a fragment of tobacco. "Yes," he answered with a very bold display indeed, "I did." He went on to say that strictly speaking he should have asked Gisborough's permission before proposing to Catherine, but that he believed that observance of this custom had grown unusual nowadays (and he was in time to prevent himself putting in a coarse laugh at this juncture). He told Gisborough, moreover, that he had not only very little money of his own, but no great prospects from his father, a successful solicitor; all the same he was not poor, as he was doing well at the bar. "You can call it beginner's luck, if you like," he said, aware that it was improper for him to issue permissions to Gisborough concerning what he might or might not call things, but aware too that these sweeping overarm strokes of his were better for the present purpose, than sliding beneath the waves, as he surely would, were he to hesitate for an instant: "and I sometimes call it that myself," he went on, "but after a couple of years you know if you've got talent, and I seem to have some of that." He sketched his war record, and how he came to wear the Military Cross. He said: "I was in a mess, and I could either run away and be court-martialled for cowardice, or stay and get a medal. So I stayed. That's about all there was to that." He spat out some more tobacco. His tongue was loosened now, and as people miraculously cured of some crippling defect are said to leap recklessly hither and thither, so Ferrers, liberated from his muteness, gave forth an uncontrolled utterance, talking rapidly and vehemently, so that in the swift career of his speech vehemence and passion sometimes occurred in inappropriate places, as when in a badly conducted orchestra the percussion lags behind the trumpets and thunder. He ran to great length. He gave Gisborough many undesired details of his regiment, and of why he had disapproved of the French wartime cus- tom of shaving guilty women, of the advantages of being related to a solicitor if you were a barrister, and of much other matter. He was a perspicacious young man, and he saw that by talking too much he might make new problems for himself. Having not yet regained natural self-control he stopped speaking abruptly, with astonish- ing effect.

Gisborough nodded.

During this recital he had been wondering whether it could be logically maintained that the mark of the truly civilized man was that he was above certain considerations of time, and notably of his own age. Here was a young man of good appearance, excellent attainments, and who was in this place for an important reason. And yet, because he was in the presence of a man much older than himself, he was entirely unable to behave naturally, or perhaps *could* only behave but with a horrible naturalness, even as he himself had done when giving rein to thoughts of mutilations, seeing them in his mind's eye performed on the blameless fellow at his side.

He turned his potato face to Ferrers, and looked him straight, though mildly, in the eyes.

"I won't inquire into your feelings," he said, following his plan to relinquish his daughter with a stoic lack of fuss, "but I think I ought to inquire into your finances. You say you are not poor. How much have you a year?"

"You know," replied Ferrers, unable as yet to make a terse statement, "Fellows at the bar, for some reason I've never understood, have a way of exaggerating their takings, and I'm no exception. I can honestly say however that I'm making enough. Not huge sums, mark you, but I'm making *money*."

"How much?"

"I average nine hundred a year at the moment. I'll go on doing that for a year or two yet. Then I'll be making much more, I hope."

"Nine hundred," said Gisborough, and there followed a long pause in which nine hundred was given what chance it had to make a good impression. "Well" — and then he added very slowly — "that seems all right."

It was with these words that Gisborough gave Catherine into the keeping of Ferrers.

Had they belonged to a jollier tradition than our own, the two men would have embraced at this high moment of their lives and shed some tears. As it was Ferrers huskily muttered something about it being very good of him, and Gisborough went quietly through his prepared speech about his feeling sure that Catherine had chosen well.

Henri brought sherry and glasses on a little tray.

Gisborough poured out sherry and before drinking gave the young man a brief serious look as he raised his glass. Other traditions would have demanded little formal speeches from them now, but they drank to the future joys of marriage in silence.

Ferrers was now in a calm though slightly complicated state. At the outset he had seen two obstacles between him and the winning post, obstacles so dreadful that, brave as he was, he had been thrown into a state of almost helpless nervousness. As he came sliding safely to earth over the first great fence his confidence returned to him in full measure, and so he rode at the second one not only without any sort of qualm, but with an exhilarating thrill, even though it was the thought of this second obstacle which had most alarmed him.

He now addressed Gisborough with the ease of one man of the world talking to another. "Might I say, Sir," he said, "how grateful I am to you for making all this so easy for me. I am very honoured that you should take me on trust."

"Catherine is a very good introduction to me," replied Gisborough with a melancholy smile.

"Ah, yes . . . That I well believe. But she is very generous, you know. I'm not an ideal son-in-law by any means."

"Only a very upright millionaire can be that."

Ferrers took a cigarette from the open box and lit it. He had a dim sense of heroism because he knew that although it was perfectly feasible for him to avoid the second obstacle, this easier course of action would involve some deception. Catherine had said that she loved him for being so honest, and honest and lovable he would be.

He laughed charmingly. "That ideal is not easily attained," he said, and then, more seriously, "I am not merely being polite, you know. I am particularly ill-suited to be the son-in-law of a great writer."

A frown for a moment lined the top of Gisborough's white blank face.

"How? I don't follow you. You mean — what?"

"I mean, Mr. Gisborough, that I am the exact opposite of a literary man. The complete and absolute antithesis."

Gisborough would have supposed that Ferrers was speaking conventionally, was merely carrying out a token abasement of cricket before culture, had he not noticed, from a certain earnest expression, that he was occupied with a serious thought. The young man was sitting in an easy attitude, with his powerful legs crossed, and a powerful foot swinging slowly. He was smiling gravely and confidently, but with an unquiet look in his eyes.

Gisborough admired simplicity of character, but he

found the simplicity of this young man in supposing that he intended his daughter for some cultivated person with whom he could converse about literature, excessive.

"Well," he said, "I never supposed that you *were* a 'literary man.' " He looked at him, puzzling.

"You'd been warned? Ah, that makes it easier," said Ferrers.

"Warned? How do you mean 'warned?' Who should 'warn' me?" Gisborough showed that he disliked Ferrers' remark. Then he continued in a more kindly fashion: "I really must not let you suppose that I only like people who share the same profession and interests as myself."

Ferrers pulled at his cigarette and laughed gently.

"I never supposed that," he said, and Gisborough saw that he had done wrong in addressing him as a child, saw too, that he had underestimated the force of his guest's return to sanity. "I was referring to the fact that I am very ill-read, quite appallingly and extraordinarily so. I read what I was told to at school, and I read enough at Oxford for a very unbrilliant degree. I have read nothing outside that at all. Nothing. I have never read for pleasure, never wanted to, and now that I have to read through a lot of papers as part of my work, I want to less than ever. I have not the least idea what Dickens or Thackeray or Sir Walter Scott wrote about. I know the name of only one poem by Milton, but I couldn't quote a single line. I think that as you write books you ought to know that about me, because it's a bit unusual."

He spoke calmly, showing no sign of agitation except for a vein which throbbed in his neck. Gisborough listened with interest. When he spoke, after a short pause, he did so in order to check the facts.

"But, as a member of a learned profession," he said, "don't you find yourself seriously handicapped by — by what you've just told me about yourself?"

"Not in the least," laughed Ferrers, "not in the very slightest! Every now and again a counsel or judge makes a literary remark and I miss it. I usually appear to have seen the point, all the same. As for being seriously handicapped — that just doesn't come into it."

Gisborough looked up at the mass of green and fading leaves. For a moment he was silent with surprise. He was used to discovering that the people he knew, even the learned ones, had often read considerably less than they appeared to have done, but almost total illiteracy, ignorance of the very nature of Scott and Thackeray, came to him as something new. He could not tell why, but this discovery gave him a faint and strange feeling of fear. He turned to Ferrers again: "You are not exaggerating, perhaps?"

"No, I'm not. Please don't think I'm anything but very sorry about it, either. I know well enough that I miss a lot of pleasure in life. It's a sort of disease, you know, this positive aversion to reading, like having no taste for food."

"Do you quite literally *never* read? What do you do on railway journeys, for example?"

"I look out of the window."

"And if it's dark?"

"I day-dream or go to sleep. Of course I read the papers — I have to."

"But never magazines?"

He read articles in weeklies occasionally, as part of his duties, so he asked: "What sort of *magazines*?"

"Oh," Gisborough replied, "the sort with stories in it." Adding with a little chuckle, "The sort in which only too many of my stories have appeared, I am ashamed to say. You know, the sort with shiny paper."

As he rose to the second fence, collecting his steed, and deftly applying his spurs, Ferrers once more made the brutal grimace which went with his determination.

"Mr. Gisborough," he said, "I think I ought to tell you that I have never read one of your stories, or novels — you write novels chiefly, don't you?"

Very primly, raising his eyebrows very high while his mouth formed itself into a small circle, Gisborough said: "Oh."

Henri came up to them and announced that lunch was ready. He then swiftly retraced his steps and once more vanished indoors. The two men walked towards the house, the younger taking care not to outstrip the older man, who moved very slowly, gliding over the expanse of turf sluggishly and gracelessly.

As they approached the house Gisborough gave Ferrers a smile to show that he did not mind.

But he did mind. He was surprised that this should be so, but he could not mistake the fact of his minding, and he wondered, as he entered the house, what the reason could be. He supposed at first that the novelty of the situation had shaken him out of his usual indifference to fame. For many years he had assumed that all the people he met had read some, if not most, of his books.

Then quite suddenly, and in the least likely circumstances, he had found that this was not true. As he looked
more closely at the shock which he had received, he saw
a deeper reason for it: namely the strange array of pos-
sibilities which this situation implied in his relationship
to Ferrers. For to the latter, who lived among educated
people, he could not possibly be utterly anonymous, as
he was to people in the street; he must be endowed with
some definite character — and with what character, how
ineptly conceived, was he perhaps pictured in the mind's
eye of this enemy of all books and reading! It followed
that Ferrers almost certainly imagined him to be a different sort of writer than he was, perhaps far greater, a
tremendous trumpet-tongued genius whose name would
live for many centuries to come; but, and this he saw as
far more likely since Ferrers had so little to compare
him with, the young man probably looked upon his
future father-in-law, and with much respect, as a mag-
nificently successful contriver of purple marvels about
sheikhs and veiled women, and even worse. In all likeli-
hood Ferrers degraded him to unimagined depths. In a
flash of speculation he fancied openings to novels which
the young man might suppose to be typical of his work.
"Cavendish St. Leger rose jerkily to his feet and hur-
riedly closed the casement . . . Outside the sea roared
implacably. . . ."

"Come on in to luncheon," he said, waving his guest
through the door.

The dining-room was a small cosy room whose walls
were covered with dark green silk. There were many

pictures hung one above the other on the wall in the conservative French fashion. The finest was a portrait by Ingres of a bearded man. Gisborough showed Ferrers to a place at the round table.

"I did not ask you," he said, "whether you wished to stay the night."

"I'm afraid my aeroplane makes that impossible," said Ferrers. "It leaves at eight in the morning from Le Bourget, and I doubt if I can catch a train from here early enough. I am unfortunately bound to leave tomorrow, as we're so busy at the end of term."

"I see. Do you know Paris?"

"This is pretty well my first visit. I dashed through once just after liberation, when I was in the army, but I didn't have time to see anything."

"Then you must go and have a first-rate dinner in Paris, and see the sights of the town. I'll give you some addresses of restaurants and cabarets."

He adjusted his glasses for eating, and then, while Ferrers helped himself to the omelette, he said: "As regards a marriage settlement. I will write to Catherine today that I am leaving that entirely to the lawyers. You'll find them very sensible. I will instruct them to arrange for Catherine to receive a thousand a year in addition to her small income. Also a small capital payment for a house."

"You are most generous. I am very grateful."

Gisborough said nothing to this, but helped himself to the omelette.

"And now," he said, "I want to know where you intend to live. Catherine tells me you have found a very nice house by the river in Cheyne Walk. Where is it? At which end?"

Ferrers was happy after his ordeal, and for the first time that day entirely at his ease, as if he were relaxing in the weighing-in room and receiving congratulations. To Gisborough's question he returned a sensible reply in a voice which was firm and manly. When asked for more details he gave them at appropriate length. His father-in-law was at last seeing the essential Ferrers, the decent reliable "sideless" natural Ferrers; and while the young man supposed that now he might have an opportunity of making a good impression, Gisborough's interest in him faded, a fact which was signalled, as people who knew him would have noticed, by a certain lengthening of his face as his hidden mouth drooped, a narrowing of his eyes, and a slight intensifying of his politeness.

"Describe the house as exactly as you can," he said, "and all the rooms. I'm interested in houses. They are one of my fads."

The young man described his future home, and how he and Catherine intended to use the rooms, in minute detail, encouraged by nods and grunts from the other, and by an appearance of good-humoured interest in his screwed-up eyes. He could not guess that Gisborough was far away from him.

Like a spy who has taken ship by stealth on the eve of war, and who now, safely settled in his cabin in the submarine, spreads out his code-books and photographs, together with maps of the friendly land whose betrayal is his business; like such a man Gisborough inwardly settled down to the task of classifying his guest in terms of convertible literary stuff.

Gisborough was a man who very rarely wrote at any great imaginative distance from his experience. Only in the case of young people did he sometimes make considerable transpositions, not because his imagination was moved by the sight of youth to unusual virtuosity, for he despised immaturity, but because people belong to humanity in general before they are old enough to have settled into the ways and habits or appearance of some particular skill.

The omelette was followed by a saddle of lamb. Conversation about the house in Cheyne Walk was finished, and so Gisborough began to ask about the life of the law courts. He wanted to know about the chief personalities, thus leading Ferrers to speak about a certain celebrated K.C. to whom he had acted as junior in a long piece of litigation involving one of the great international oil companies.

"I could not understand," said Gisborough, "why judgment went against the company. They seemed to have acted entirely within their rights, and even generously. Was the judgment considered sound by lawyers?"

"Oh, perfectly."

"I only saw the reports in the papers, but I followed them with great care. I'm a shareholder. To me the judgment was inexplicably harsh, and I have wanted to know ever since what the explanation was."

"Well . . . It was a very complicated case and to give you the explanation would take rather a long time, I'm afraid."

Ferrers noticed Gisborough open and then close his mouth, as though in sudden surprise. But all he said was:

"Please tell me about it. I'm very curious to know."

The spy in the submarine had found the solution of his problem.

Gisborough remembered that, according to Catherine, the meeting between Ferrers and her mother had been a success. Catherine had given him this news without any comment, and he understood. Since his former wife, who was called Vera, liked everyone, she naturally liked Ferrers. Gisborough saw her ever-youthful form once more, and her tender and pitiful smile. He had not met her for nearly ten years, he had seen her at a distance, a year ago in London. He assumed that he would have to meet her again now.

She was a child of Nature. When he first set eyes on her in the year 1911 children of Nature were still a fairly new invention. She was very young in those days, and it was possible that in her elaborate display of natural spirits there was something genuine. She had ways of throwing back her head and using her eyes at what must have been an uncomfortably acute angle, of laughing deeply and slyly and softly, of shedding tears at unexpected moments, and of rushing over mown grass in her bare feet. Her long hair streamed in the wind whenever this could be arranged. Some of her elders said that she reminded them of haunting things by Walter Crane.

He sat next to her at dinner soon after their first meeting. She spoke to him about his writing without any apology or fuss, telling him what she found wrong with his composition and ideas, in the fashion of a lovely child which has not yet learned the wicked arts of polite deception. When she seemed to realize that she was being over-bold, she tried to make up for her misbehaviour by bashful praise. There was something very touching about this clumsy attempt to play the tactful grown-up. Throughout this performance her parents cast anxious glances at her and Gisborough, whenever they could spare them from their other guests, in order to ascertain whether the rising young author was offended, and they were gratified when they saw that he was entranced by the nymph, just as they and their friends were. As he talked to her by the mellow light of the red-shaded candles, he thought her not only delicious in her child-like way, but intelligent too.

Her father, who was called Turner, was managing director of a large bookselling business with over fifty branches in London and the Midlands. His main office was in London and his house was in Hammersmith. He was a man of considerable means. In the first days of his courtship of Vera, Gisborough feared that Mr. Turner might have high social ambitions for his daughter, but rather to his surprise he found that this was not so. When Turner saw that Gisborough was in love he did what he could to encourage a marriage. Long before Gisborough asked Vera to marry him, or had even decided to ask her, Turner treated him as one of the family.

This period of love and courtship did not begin till 1913, just after the publication of Gisborough's novel

Friend Remembered. Vera had always attracted him, but now that she seemed to want him, now that she gave him a vision of consummated love and happiness, he fell deeply in love with her. Long after, he told himself that he should have seen that her passion for him was shallow because its first manifestation coincided so precisely with his first considerable literary success. He reproached himself too at this later time, for not having seen through the wiles with which she sustained her role of the child of Nature. He reached the conclusion that love is blind.

They would have married in the Autumn of 1914, but in August they decided to wait till the end of the war which was reliably predicted for 1915. Both Gisborough and the Turners had the advantage of knowing people in high official positions who could advise them expertly on such matters. Gisborough spent most of the next five years attached to the British Military Mission in Paris, while Vera became an officer in the W.R.N.S. She sometimes went to Paris in the course of her duties, just as he sometimes came to London. They took leave together when they could. At the end of 1917 they got married.

The trouble about Nature is that she is at once deceptive and precise. Posing as a rural beauty, pure and simple, she hides the fact that she can live just as lustily in the squalor of the town as amid the flowers of the country, and that she is ceaselessly occupied in debt-collecting, a haggler for the last farthing who can never be propitiated by any other sacrifice. Poor Vera really had become a child of Nature by this time, very different indeed from the innocent faun who looked sideways in imaginary forests, though she still followed the practice of doing this, and of throwing back her head, and all the rest of it. The fiercest of the goddesses, in the course of her tireless dunning operations, had taken full possession of Vera, and so she was condemned to live the life of an animal in cities built by the craft of man's supernatural mind. The very poor are in the same sore strait through no fault of their own. When Gisborough married Vera he found he had entered a world in which all relationships had long ago relapsed into a state of brutal impulse. He was expected to adopt a large family-in-law of lovers. These men, who had a sort of gross honesty about them in that it did not occur to any of them to make a secret of what they did, used her, as she used them, by way of convenience. Neither by argument, nor by appeals to her imagination, could he change her ways, or even suggest to her that her ways ought to be changed, for Nature, into whose bosom she had thrown herself, is merciful as well as exacting, and she had made Vera's predicament bearable by administering large doses of her most sovereign anodyne. Vera had grown stupid in the way only very wretched people can. She had the frightful stupidity of slum-dwellers. None of this was visible to most of her friends and acquaintances. You needed to love her to discover her degradation. Gisborough sometimes wondered whether her father, an intelligent and observant man, had encouraged her marriage because he knew what had happened to her.

When the war ended, and they were both demobilized, Gisborough hoped, in the simple way of thought he followed in what concerned his private life, that the more ordered routine of peacetime would allow his marriage to grow into a normal human shape. Unfortunately he struck a patch of time which made for an immense aggravation of his problem instead of solution. Children of Nature, aforetime a small esoteric body, came into their own, multiplied, inherited the earth, for a season. What chance had Vera in a world which found an ideal in "Youth"? She identified herself with "Youth." She took up Youth's cause and proclaimed this alliance by those careful excesses of behaviour, typical of the times, which were supposed by many leading thinkers to express some philosophy. Vera believed herself to be taking part in a tremendous epic struggle between a brave new world and an old, corrupt, and outworn one. Such a struggle was often mentioned by the people she knew, and she presumed that this was it. It never occurred to her that she was taking part in an act of surrender, by no means such a one as is unique in history. It never said so in the few books she read, or in the great quantities of talk she heard, and she was far too simple to work out any idea on her own. It is doubtful whether Vera would ever have had a child, because she believed that child-bearing belonged to the outworn world, and that the "third sex" which, she had been told, was then emerging, should be encouraged to "realize itself" by a world-wide female strike against the pangs of gestation and birth; had it not been that her father, who was close to death, decided to leave £10,000 to his grandson or granddaughter should he be so blessed. Then she bore Catherine. The measure of her dullness was that this event made a small impression on her. When, a year later, Gisborough attempted to divorce her, she showed that her cult of brutishness had not made her brave. She insisted, with rage and tears, that the initiative in the case must lie with her. She even appealed to Gisborough's sense of chivalry to enable her to perjure herself into the status of innocent party against her husband. He was so glad to be free of her that he agreed to her wishes and did not defend himself. The law gave her part custody of her child, but she gladly surrendered her share later. So ended nine years of marriage in which he had known hardly an hour of happiness. He remembered, much to his shame, how he had secretly hoped for Vera's death when Catherine was born.

He had only spoken to her once since then, and that was because they met by accident in London.

As related above, he had accused himself, after marriage, of foolishness in not seeing that her love for him was only a contemptible abasement before his success. As time passed, after his divorce, he began to doubt whether this estimate was just. She often sent messages of affection to him through friends, and he heard through these same friends of how she spoke about him: affectionately, remorsefully, and in the pompous tones of one who acts the tragedian. He grew to recognize two truths which explained much about her: that one may act a part without being insincere, and that one may betray one's best friend, not because one's nature is treacherous, but because it is silly. Vera destroyed her husband's middle years because she followed the herd more than one should. People do not go astray like demons, but like sheep. He grew to recognize that she had given him all the love in her heart. If his own heart had been a great one he would have been moved by the immensity of this offering; but because it was small he could only note, with contempt, that this offered love was not according to his taste. In consequence he found no difficulty in repelling her advances with effective cruelty. The advances grew timid but they did not cease.

By the late nineteen thirties it had become plain to all her contemporaries that she was a fool. She became "dated" because she lacked the finished hypocrisy necessary to a life of long fashionability; she became widely known as the authoress of amusingly stupid remarks; the dropping process set in. However she was not dropped by every one. Although she was now over fifty she still had the physical charms which excite passionate desire. These excitements were growing rare, but they gave her sufficiently numerous lovers to hide her failure from herself. She did not know, of course, that whereas aforetime men liked to be known as her lovers, they now kept this fact secret for fear of being mocked. More than of old, they used her in a purely animal way for their needs. Having lived like a sheep, she loved and was loved in the same woolly fashion.

What she needed most urgently was someone fresh to her world who knew nothing about her. She needed respect. Perhaps Ferrers, who knew nothing about her, could give her this needed respect. . . .

And now as he sat with the young man at lunch, Gisborough saw the construction of a piece with a beautiful curve passing through different points of view. He saw the whole of his design spread out before him, some parts even in detail. He saw an opening in expression of a sentiment usually reserved for the conclusions of stories: the new light shed on events and situations by the fresh mind of a fresh generation.

He knew well the temptation, which sometimes comes over men, to rely on the supposed strength and innocence of the young. He remembered in the period immediately after the First Great War a tendency, which he had often been inclined to follow, which led people to ascribe to the young a mysterious wisdom and loftiness of soul, because their hands were not soiled with the blood of their fellow men, whereas older hands were. He guessed that the same temptation existed in the nineteen forties. By imagining Ferrers only a little younger than he was, he saw him, very easily, as that idol of father-spirits too weak for the vastness of modern responsibilities and guilt, and without much difficulty he could see himself as the unconfident and worshipping father. Here, splendid in unstained youth, in the bright vigour of a guiltless generation, was the Interceder.

The action commences when the two main figures of this story enter the packed church where the younger generation are to be married. For the first time since their separation the father and Vera stand side by side in the front pew of a large rich dark London neo-Gothic Church. In one main and necessary respect the imagined Vera is an improvement on the living one: she loves her child with the only deep and sincere emotion in her being. Nature is represented as having left that most holy part of her, the maternal impulse, untouched by the stultification of her soul, for Gisborough knew that pure fatuosity is as undepictable as pure genius.

As he stands there amid the ancient fluster and poetry of weddings, the father wonders why he should feel as though this ceremony has happened before, somewhat as in the way we have an unearthly sensation of duality in experience when the two sides of the brain are not working in unison. Then he understands. The feeling of sadness which now oppresses him, at parting with his child, is a dim reflection of the grief and pain he imposed on his wife when he divorced her; for he did this, in his fictional character taking the initiative against her, so that her impropriety was exposed in the ugliest light, and so that by the decision of the court she lost all guardianship of the child. In the church it came to him at last that the retribution he had obtained from the law was more than any human being has the right to exact from another. He had been guilty of the hideous sin of insisting on everything due to him; and as the organ growls and peals he turns to her and looks at her face for the first time for twenty years. She is still young, still desirable, still helplessly simple, so he guesses. With a sudden shock he realizes what he ought to have realized as soon as he turned: that she is looking at him, and must have been doing so for some time. In an access of emotion he holds her hand for a second, and whispers the fatal words: "I'm sorry."

The fictional Ferrers is as heavily decked with charm and graces as can be contrived without descending to lush excesses of description. He is not a lawyer; he follows the far more thrilling career of politics. Gisborough belonged to the generation of imaginative writers who, when they wished to portray sympathetic politicians, described them as members of the Labour Party, and when they wished to portray ridiculous or evil politicians, first labelled them Conservative. The only sympathetic portraits of Conservatives allowed by these conventions were closely influenced by certain heroes in the works of Tolstoy: namely they showed idealists whose aspirations were accepted as useful assets by colleagues who secretly derided them. Gisborough well understood the harmful artificiality of these canons, but he felt too old to break new ground here. For the sake of having a splendid marriage the young man must be Conservative, and Gisborough found the old pattern useful since the element of idealism, all the more moving because it is doomed to failure in public life, must be the mainspring.

Ferrers is the Interceder. He is absolutely addicted to interceding. He begins on his mother-in-law soon after his marriage. Vera likes every one, and she takes on Ferrers with all her usual gush. But she cannot keep it up; not in the presence of that sincere young face, of those grave youthful eyes which see through appearances with the courage of one who has not yet been defeated by Life. Unexpectedly to herself, but less so to fictional Ferrers, she breaks down one day and confides to her future son-in-law the depths and extent of her misery. He sees her without her coquetry, in the remorse and loneliness of her age. And he is touched. And he believes that in her real self she is one deserving of compassion because she has loved much. Ferrers takes up her cause because he believes, in the insolent confidence of his all-hallowed youth, that his mission is to act as the saviour of this Magdalene. He determines to try to effect a reconciliation, for he knows that Vera needs the respect and love of her lawful husband. He knows too that she can have it after he has heard from Vera of the episode at his wedding.

The Interceder uses an argument which is irresistible to the youth-worshipping father. He tells him this: the world lies in ruins around him, and all men and women over a certain age, particularly prominent men such as the father, bear some part of the blame for the carnage and havoc. He, the father, can feel forgiven for his share of the blood of innocents, because his cause was more righteous than the other. And yet he himself, who accepts all this forgiveness complacently and as his due, cannot forgive in his turn, has no kindness to spare, not even for a woman who loves him. He refuses kindness to her because she has injured him. She has not destroyed his life as he has done to her, or as, in his country's name, he has joined in doing to countless others. She has hurt his vanity, nothing more than that. The father listens to these arguments of guiltless youth, and moved by a sudden rash impulse to do one generous action before it is too late, he is reconciled to Vera, and remarries her.

They live unhappily ever after. What poor fictional Ferrers did not know was that acts of splendid generosity can only be done by splendid people. The father was not deficient in intelligence but in high purpose and virtue, and for that reason his attempt to perform a tremendous act of selflessness was useless and destructive. Vera on her side was deficient in every quality, good and bad, except self-regard, and maternal love which did not affect the issue; and so she had no right to accept the superhuman sacrifice which Gisborough offered her. Between them they proved that without charity it is possible for people to distribute their wealth to the poor and yet remain nothing.

Vera was unused to security or success. She was quite unfitted to possess them suddenly. She grew vain and selfish in a gross manner which was repulsive even by the standards of the gross world to which she belonged. The father watched her appalled. He found many reasons for growing cantankerous. Because he found it physically horrifying to occupy in late middle-age the contemptible position he had occupied in youth, be became haunted by dread of becoming old, long before his time. He soon associated his second marriage with the most horrible of calamities, that of growing old comically. There was truly no escape for him except the escape of death. He looked with self-pity at what he had bought by his immense act of noble kindness. As the years drew on he amused his embittered mind with thoughts of murder. But he did not murder; his cruel daydreams were only first signs of a premature second childishness: Vera, strengthened by a renewal of her coarse vitality, showed no sign of dying.

The conclusion was too distant to be seen clearly by Gisborough in this moment of first improvisation: but he saw clearly the supreme object of this tale; the father, at last obtained revenge for the second marriage by conveying his bitterness, first unconsciously and then intentionally, to the daughter he loved. She then began to look with bitterness at her husband, fictional Ferrers, because he had ruined the last years of her beloved father. She grows to hate him with a savage fury far exceeding anything between the father and Vera. Thus far Gisborough could see. For the rest he relied on a return of the demon who sits on the feathers of pens.

When they had finished drinking their liqueurs, Gisborough took Ferrers for a stroll round his garden, after which he conducted him to the trout stream in order to show him the occurrence of a fine pool in a beautiful passage. Their conversation was easy throughout, and throughout Gisborough seemed anxious to hear what the young man had to say. So, rather to his surprise, Ferrers did most of the talking, and Gisborough seemed interested in everything he had to tell him. Only once did his attention appear to wander, when Ferrers asked him about the sixty-pound salmon he had caught in Norway. They were standing by the pool, watching for fish in its clear depths, while Gisborough gently prodded the earth with his walking stick. He seemed not to hear, and when he had repeated the question Ferrers wondered whether the salmon was a painful memory, and how this could possibly be. But Gisborough was again occupied with the scene in the church, the shock when the father realized how long the mother had been watching him, the father's fatal words. Then quickly he registered the question.

"I'm sorry. Oh, yes . . . yes. The salmon! I had almost forgotten . . . I caught him in the Nordesfjord in

1932. He was a vast weight. But did you know that those very large salmon are not so difficult as the twenty-five pounders? The fat ones are lazy and don't fight hard. Like men, I suppose. Have you fished for salmon?"

"I have in Ireland."

"In Ireland. Have you? I have only fished in Scotland and Norway. Tell me about fishing in Ireland."

They walked slowly back along the path which took them once more to his garden, then up and down the lawn for a while. Because of the English guest, tea was brought out to a table under the tree at a quarter-past four. At five o'clock a car arrived to take the young man back to the station. As he picked up his hat from the table he took care that Gisborough should not see the fat brown book he had with him, but Gisborough had seen it as they came into the hall. From a great distance he could recognize the volume of his collected short stories. They shook hands, and Gisborough stayed at the door to wave good-bye to him.

"I take it all back," said Ferrers to Catherine. "Your father's a poppet. You were quite right. We got on like a house on fire. And what's more I told him."

"Told him what?"

"Told him I couldn't read. Told him I didn't know the name of one of his damned books."

"Did he mind? I'm sure he didn't."

"He said 'Oh' and then laughed. Oddly enough he liked me better after that. Queer, isn't it? He wanted to know everything about me, and he made me talk such a dickens of a lot that when I got back to Paris I was parched. I had to have two champagne cocktails running. I like your father. I really do."

"He's a darling."

"I like your mother, too. What a pity they can't see each other's good points."

"Papa has told me they were terribly unhappy together."

"So you've told me. Inexplicable . . . Well, I suppose they know their own minds."

"Yes, they certainly do." She changed the conversation and asked him what he had done in Paris.

"I missed you in Paris, darling," he said. He took hold of her and kissed her with a marvellous sense of achievement; of his own strength and success.

Mr. Gisborough was drinking brandy out of a handsome tulip-shaped glass. He was sitting in an elegant basket chair in front of his drawing-room, on the little stone-flagged terrace which was lighted from behind by the glow of the lamp through the open French windows, from above by the glitter of the universe. His long writing career was coming to an end. That he recognized quite clearly now, and he faced the fact with courage. No more would a demon sit on the feather of his pen, never, never again would he work with burning hissing metal; if he remained, he must remain tinting plaster in the hidden room, for it was all he could do, but he would be wise to stop before his hand or eye grew unreliable. He would be wisest to accept old age, if possible with a grave joy. For a few hours he had been captivated by an illusion of being made young again, of being gifted with strong idiosyncratic passion, of finding in this passion the energy which could fill his words with life. It had seemed to him that in the dry hollow depths of his heart he had discovered a living emotion; hideous, writhing, loathsome to touch, but living none the less. There had flashed before his mind the vision of a tale worthy to celebrate the awful sentiment of hatred for his hateful wife which he had found thus hidden away. But soon, when he began to organize his sentiment to fit into a design, he discovered that it depended on only apparent fire which, in the chill of serious examination, went out swiftly. He did not care a button about Vera, whether she was happy, or unhappy, dead or alive. He had long ago spent what joy and grief he had for her; of that he had not one scrap left for literary use. If he could feel anything about Vera at all, it was only wonder that he could at any time have felt or thought strongly about that pitifully foolish woman. What had moved him that afternoon, he saw now, was a perfectly childish sense of pique against Ferrers. Inexplicably to himself he found that he continued to mind that this self-confident and handsome, this successful, rather vulgarly attractive young man *had never read his books*. He did not wish to mind this, but he did mind. The whole purpose of the story which he had told himself that afternoon was not directed against Vera, but against Ferrers. He wanted, entirely against his will and judgment, to expose, degrade, and embitter Ferrers in the most painful imaginable way. He wanted to make of him a repulsive mock-Saviour. And that desire was passing too.

He drank some more brandy, and that unearthly liquid soothed him. He looked at the stars and smiled. "Well, at all events," he said to himself, "I can still feel some vanity."

A NOTE ON THE TYPE IN WHICH
THIS BOOK IS SET

This book was set on the Linotype in Janson, *a re-cutting made direct from the type cast from matrices made by Anton Janson some time between 1660 and 1687.*

Of Janson's origin nothing is known. He may have been a relative of Justus Janson, a printer of Danish birth who practised in Leipzig from 1614 to 1635. Some time between 1657 and 1668 Anton Janson, a punch-cutter and type-founder, bought from the Leipzig printer Johann Erich Hahn the type-foundry which had formerly been a part of the printing house of M. Friedrich Lankisch. Janson's types were first shown in a specimen sheet issued at Leipzig about 1675. Janson's successor, and perhaps his son-in-law, Johann Karl Edling, issued a specimen sheet of Janson types in 1689. His heirs sold the Janson matrices in Holland to Wolffgang Dietrich Erhardt, of Leipzig.

The book was composed, printed, and bound by The Plimpton Press, Norwood, Massachusetts. Designed by Harry Ford.